A Simple Piece of Mind

Simon Quellen Field

A Simple Piece of Mind

Cover art by Simon Quellen Field

A Kinetic MicroScience Book

Published by Kinetic MicroScience, LLC

19395 Montevina Road

Los Gatos, California, 95033

www.scitoys.com

ISBN 978-0-9822104-3-7

First edition: December 2009

To Whom It May Concern

Chapter One

The funny little man was looking at me.

Since my accident, I usually could not recognize faces. People were blobs of indistinct movement, who disappeared if they stopped moving. My brain was no longer able to process them. At the clinic, everyone wore nametags and I can read just fine. Nametags on blobs of moving shape made it easy to tell what was a person and what was a potted plant. That made it easier not to have long fruitless conversations with potted plants. But here in the coffee house, only Amy wore a nametag.

I recognized the funny little man. I could tell he was looking at me. I felt like I should know his name, but no name came to mind. I could not tell what was funny about him. That he was funny at all was quite interesting. That he was someone I could recognize was amazing. I sat there, amazed. I don't think I had been amazed since the accident. It was a funny feeling. I don't recall having any feelings since the accident, so maybe all of them are funny. I like that word. Funny. So much friendlier than strange, or weird. It's much better to be funny.

I've been funny for over a year now. I wear a funny hat. It covers the scars on my bald head, and it has batteries that power the chip in my brain that is trying to connect the various parts across the damaged areas. It connects the chip to the computer in my backpack that does most of the work. The computer on the table in front of me is just for surfing the web.

I raised my hand and touched my funny hat. The funny little man did not reach up and touch his hat. I don't think he had a hat. But at least I knew I wasn't facing a mirror. It would make some sense if the first face I could recognize would be my own. The funny little man kept looking at me. I don't remember people doing that before the accident. Children looked at funny people that way. Maybe this was a child. I smiled, and made a tiny wave with my hand. The funny little man did not react.

Perhaps I was being stared at by a potted plant. I considered whether my brain was just confused, triggering a signal of recognition when there was nothing to recognize. Or maybe I was facing a portrait of someone famous. Someone everyone would recognize, even someone with only half a brain.

I heard the bus arrive. I looked up, and I could read the words on the side of the bus. Words help. When things are labeled, I can read what they are. Sounds are good too, if I can remember what sound goes with what. I know the bus sound.

"Time to go, Jerry." I knew that voice. It was somebody's sister. I looked around for the nametag, but didn't see it.

"Here we go," the voice said again, and the lid to my laptop started to close onto my fingers. I looked up and saw the nametag. Mary Elizabeth. I don't know whose sister she is. She comes with the bus.

I stood up, holding onto the laptop tightly. The heavy backpack wanted to pull me over backwards, but I have learned how to keep from falling down. That's why I get to go places on the bus.

I walked to the label that said *This door to remain open during business hours.* It wasn't open. Sometimes the labels are wrong. But I remembered how to open the door, even with the laptop computer in one hand. I'm getting better every day.

Larry was already on the bus. Sometimes Larry has a nametag, but I can tell it's Larry because he's big, he always is yellow, and he smells different. I sat down in the seat across from Larry, far enough away that the smell wasn't unpleasant. Mary Elizabeth sat down in the seat in front of Larry.

"I saw a strange little man today," I said. "He wasn't a president or a rock star, but he wasn't a mirror."

Nobody said anything. Sometimes people don't understand. But I am patient with them, even when they are slow. Larry is very slow, but he seems to understand better than Mary Elizabeth.

"He wasn't a potted plant," I said.

"You're a funny guy, Jerry," Mary Elizabeth said. I could not see her nametag anymore, but she was black and white, and everything else was in color, so I knew where she was.

"I know," I said. "I'm sorry. But we're fixing that."

"He wasn't a potted plant," Larry explained to Mary Elizabeth. Larry didn't have a chip in his head. But he understood things that Mary Elizabeth didn't understand. He never had an accident. He was just slow.

"I'm sure he wasn't, dear," Mary Elizabeth said. The bus started to move. I could read the signs over the businesses as we passed them by. They were always the same. Except for *Don't walk*. Sometimes that one changed. I knew what that meant. But I don't walk, even when it says *Walk*. Sometimes the labels are wrong.

"Will we have Jell-O tonight?" Larry asked Mary Elizabeth. "I like Jell-O. It wiggles. I like it when it wiggles."

Mary Elizabeth turned around in her seat to look back at Larry. "There's Jell-O every night, Larry," she said.

Larry was silent for a while. "Not on Sundays," he said. "On Sundays there's ice cream. Ice cream Sundays." He sounded upset. Larry can get upset. I don't know how to get upset. When Larry gets upset, bad things can happen. Bad things are against the rules.

"Don't worry," I said. "You can have ice cream sundaes on any day of the week. But we never do. We always have Jell-O. Tonight we are having Jell-O."

The bus stopped at a red light. Some things I remember just fine. I know traffic rules. I remember driving a car. I don't remember any of the businesses on this street from before the accident. I don't think I was ever on this street before the accident. I remember going on the bus to the coffee house, but I don't remember any of the signs on the way. If I read the signs out loud, I can remember them. But I always forget the colors.

The bus stopped at the clinic. Larry got out first, and Mary Elizabeth waited for me to stand up. She always leaves the bus last. I held onto my laptop computer and walked carefully down the steps. I have to be careful on steps. One time I slipped and my hat fell off, and I couldn't think anymore. I'm not supposed to let my hat fall off. Only the doctors in the clinic are supposed to take my hat off.

I knew we were at the clinic because the sign said *Leo Finklestein Neurology Research Center* and that's what it always said when we got to the clinic. We went inside and I knew which way to go, but Mary Elizabeth started going a different way. "This way, Jerry," she said. "They need you in the lab."

Seymour was already in the lab when we got there. He has a problem with his memory, and he never remembers people. He remembers a whole lot of things, and some of them really happened, but everybody he sees is new to him.

"Hi there," he said, reaching over to turn my nametag so he could see it. "Jerry Monaghan," he said, reading the tag. "I'm Seymour Barnswallow," he said, holding his nametag up for me to see. "Inventor. One of these days, you'll own a Barnswallow and you'll tell all your friends you actually met the guy who invented it. It's gonna change the world, I tell you."

Doctor Davis and Doctor Wilson were setting up the big machine that looks inside people's heads. Seymour loves machines. "Is that a Lauterbur?" he asked.

Doctor Davis looked up. "A what?"

"A Lauterbur. Uses big magnets to align atomic nuclei and then listens to the noise they make when they get hit by a radio pulse." Seymour liked explaining things.

"You mean an MRI machine," Doctor Wilson said.

Seymour shook his head. "That's not a name. That's just a plain old description. Things should be named after their inventors. Like Paul Lauterbur. He got a Nobel prize for inventing what you just called an MRI machine."

Doctor Davis looked surprised. He's used to slow people in the lab. Or doctors. "Well, it's like an MRI machine," he said. "It's a phased array echoplanar imaging system for functional MRI." I could see him reading the side of the machine.

"And you think you're going to go around calling it that all day?" Seymour said. "Find out who invented it. Then you can call it a Wisenheimer or a Johnson. Save you lots of time."

Larry and Mary Elizabeth walked into the lab. Larry had heard the last part of the conversation. "What's a Johnson?" he asked.

"The big machine that looks inside people's heads," I said.

"Oh, yeah. I knew that," Larry said.

"For example," Seymour continued. "Take your common intermittent windshield wipers. Everybody knows they were invented by Robert Kearns. They made a movie about that. But do people say 'turn on the Kearns' when it starts raining? Heck no. They say 'windshield wipers'. Waste of time. And not even accurate, because if it's just sprinkling a little bit, you don't turn on the windshield wipers, you turn on the intermittent windshield wipers, and that's even harder to say. Just call them the Kearns. Save a lot of time, I tell you."

Larry nodded vigorously. "Yeah. Save a lot of time."

Doctor Wilson walked over to me. "Hi there, Jerry," he said. "Time to charge your hat."

He led me over to the gurney with the straps, and helped me lie down on it. Mary Elizabeth helped him fasten the straps around my arms and legs, and across my chest. "Relax," Mary Elizabeth said, pushing down on my legs. They resisted. This happens every time they say they are going to charge my hat. I can't control my legs, and my stomach gets hard, and it takes two of them to strap me down. I don't know why that is. I can control my legs just fine at the coffee house, or in the bus. Things started to look funny as the tears came. Those only come when they charge my hat too.

"There we go," Doctor Wilson said. "Everything is ready. Are you ready, Jerry?"

"I'm ready," I said. My stomach got really tight when I said it, and the words came out funny. I like that word. Funny.

Doctor Wilson reached up and removed my hat. The world went away. Somewhere, someone was screaming.

Chapter Two

The straps hurt my arms. My arms always hurt when they put my hat back on. Mary Elizabeth straightened my hat, and started undoing the straps. If she had started with my arms, I could have helped, but she started with my legs, and worked up to my chest. When my arms were free, I rubbed where it hurt.

I was very hungry. I was about to ask what time it was, but I realized I knew the exact time. It was a new feeling. I sat still and wondered at the seconds passing by.

"My brain is growing," I said.

"I should hope so," Mary Elizabeth said. "That's kind of the whole point of the program. You keep taking your pills, and it should keep on growing."

My stomach gurgled. The seconds ticked by as I stood up and followed Mary Elizabeth out into the hallway.

"I think my brain is talking to the chip in my head," I said. "It knows what time it is."

Mary Elizabeth kept walking. "It's breakfast time," she said, and we walked past the big windows looking out at the garden, and past the big doors that led outside. The cafeteria is on the other side of the garden.

Larry was already there, sitting at a table with Madeline. It was hard to see her name tag from a distance, but her name is longer than everybody else's, so I didn't have to actually read it.

Madeline has trouble keeping her brain working. Sometimes it just stops in the middle of something, and she just sits there until it starts back up. Sometimes it happens in the middle of a sentence when she's talking. When she starts back up, she just finishes the sentence. Sometimes she gets surprised when the person she was talking to isn't there anymore. Sometimes that makes her cry. I always wait until she's back. It's not good to make people cry.

Mary Elizabeth left me at the counter and went back the way we had come. I picked up a tray and walked along the counter, putting lots of scrambled eggs and bacon on my plate. I was very hungry. I took my tray over to sit with Larry and Madeline.

"I didn't get dinner last night," I said. "I'm very hungry."

Madeline looked up at me. I can see people's eyes, their noses, their mouths, and all the rest of their parts, but the parts are just parts, they don't all fit together to make a face. I can remember being able to see faces, but I can't remember any faces. But sometimes I can tell when someone is looking at me, or looking at someone else.

"They didn't let you have dinner?" she asked.

I swallowed a big bite of eggs. "They took my hat off when we got back yesterday afternoon. Mary Elizabeth put it back on this morning. My hat was off for fifteen hours, twelve minutes, and forty two seconds."

Madeline picked up a piece of bacon. "That sucks," she said. "They treat you like some kind of lab rat or something. They don't care about things like whether you get dinner. That's just not right."

Larry nodded vigorously. "That's not right. We had Jell-O last night."

Madeline was quiet. I could not tell if her brain was turned on or not. I waited until she moved her hand.

"I learned something new today," I said. "I can tell exactly what time it is. My chip has a clock in it."

Madeline smiled. I can tell when someone is smiling. Their mouth changes. "That could be useful. I should get one of those. Then I'd know how long I was gone." She looked at her wristwatch. She looked at it for a long time, but her other hand was moving, so I knew her brain was still switched on.

"I learned something new yesterday," Larry said. He looked at Madeline expectantly, but her hand had stopped moving. He looked at me. We waited.

"What did you learn, Larry?" Madeline said, her hand moving again.

"Doctor Wilson has a big Johnson," Larry said.

Madeline smiled. "I'll bet he does. When did you make this discovery?"

"Yesterday. When we were in the room where they take off Jerry's hat. Seymour was there, and he forgets things, so I have to remember things for him. So I remembered it was a Johnson as soon as it came out of Seymour's mouth."

Madeline looked over at me. "Were you there? Was your hat still on?"

I nodded. "It was that or a Wisenheimer."

Larry nodded again, enthusiastically. "Doctor Louise let's me play with hers sometimes, but Doctor Wilson's is much bigger."

"Doctor Louise? You mean Louise Roberts? She lets you play with hers?"

Larry nodded again. "We play games. It's for learning. But I like the Xbox better."

Someone came over and put their tray down on the table and pulled out a chair. When he sat down, I could read his nametag.

"Hi Seymour," I said.

He looked up at me. "Do I know you?" he asked. "How do you know my name?"

I pointed at his shirt. "I read nametags," I said.

He looked down at the tag. "Oh, quite right. Hi there. I'm Seymour Barnswallow, inventor. I invent things. All kinds of things."

Madeline looked over at Seymour. "Larry was just telling us what you and Doctor Wilson were doing yesterday."

"The big Johnson," Larry said. "Remember?"

Seymour looked at Larry for a moment. "Oh, yes! I've seen bigger, though. That one, you can only get the head in. Tight fit."

Madeline stopped moving. Seymour didn't seem to notice.

"You know," Seymour said, "Inventor's notice things. Always thinking. Look at this plate. You know how people on diets try to count calories? Why not just weigh their food? You could make a plate with a scale in it. You push a button, and it weighs your food, and adds it to the day's total. Then you weigh yourself on the bathroom scale the next day, and if you don't like the answer, don't eat as much the next day. See? Always thinking."

Madeline looked up, then looked at her wristwatch. "I'm sorry," she said, "Push a button on what?"

"On the scale built into your plate," Seymour said, poking his finger on an imaginary button on the side of his plate. "We could call it the Barnswallow."

"Wouldn't it get kind of messed up in the dishwasher?" Madeline asked.

Seymour frowned. "Gotta work on that. Yup, needs work."

"You could call it a Don'tSwallow," Madeline said. Madeline was very smart. She used to be a physics professor before her brain started skipping.

"I recognized someone yesterday," I said. "Without a nametag."

Madeline put her fork down. "Really? That's great! Who was it?"

"I don't know," I said.

Seymour stopped poking his plate. "I thought you said you recognized him."

"I think I did," I said. "I saw his face. A whole face, not just the pieces. He was looking at me. A funny little man."

No one spoke for a moment. Madeline moved her head, so I knew she was still thinking.

"What was funny about him?" Larry asked.

I thought about that. "I don't know," I said. "He was just funny. Maybe it was because he had a face, and no one else did."

"But you saw a whole face," Madeline said. "That's great! You're getting better. The pills and the chip and the therapy, they must be working!"

Seymour looked up from his plate. "Hi," he said. "I'm Seymour Barnswallow, inventor."

Chapter Three

After breakfast, it was time for my exercises. There's a special room, with lots of computers, and they talk to the computer in my backpack while I look at pictures. When a picture makes sense, I poke a button. Most pictures don't make sense. Sometimes a picture makes my stomach get hard and my legs cramp. Once a picture made my mouth water like it does just before breakfast, but I couldn't figure out why. It didn't have any food in the picture.

The exercises make me tired. I sat in front of the screen for five hours, fourteen minutes, and thirty-seven seconds, and my legs hurt, and my eyes hurt, and I got really hungry again. People came into the room and left the room, and then Mary Elizabeth came in and it was time to go on the bus again. She had to help me stand up. My legs didn't work right until I was halfway down the hall. It was hard not to fall down.

Larry was already on the bus. He really likes the bus. The bus takes him to the zoo and to the movies and to the park where people walk their dogs. Larry really likes dogs. The bus takes me to the coffee house. Then it takes Mary Elizabeth and Larry to somewhere else.

The coffee house is a good place for me because my backpack can talk to the Internet there. The people at the clinic can see what my backpack is doing even when I'm sitting in a chair in the coffee house. They like that. That's why they let me go to the coffee house. They don't let me go to the zoo.

There is food at the coffee house. When I don't get lunch at the clinic, I get food at the coffee house. I don't get coffee. The coffee house has a big menu board behind the counter. All of the food and drinks have prices, and I can read the menu. Today, as I read the menu the chip in my head adds up all the prices. It never did that before. My brain has learned how to tell the chip about prices and money. My pocket has $23.37 in it. That is not enough to buy all the things on the menu. I can buy 4.46674312 percent of the menu. I would need 22.3876765 times as much money to buy one of each item.

I have a lot of money in the bank. After my accident my insurance company put a lot of money there. And it gets bigger every month, from my disability checks, and the money the clinic pays me to be a research subject. I can use my laptop computer to find out how much money I have in the bank. But I have enough money in my pocket to buy enough food to make my stomach full again.

Amy was behind the counter. I ordered a quiche and a glass of milk. The tip jar had $7.52 in it. If I order three small chocolates, my total will come to $5.89. That will leave me $17.48. I can then put $2.48 into the tip jar, and the tip jar will have $10, and my pocket will have $15. I ordered the chocolates, and counted out $2.48 into the tip jar.

"Thank you, Jerry," Amy said. She paused. "You never tip. You feeling rich today?"

"I have fifteen dollars" I said, pointing to the three five-dollar bills on the counter. "You have ten dollars," I said, pointing to the tip jar. "I am 150 percent richer than you are."

She laughed. "You're funny, Jerry."

"I know," I said. "But I'm getting better every day."

I took my food over to my usual table. The coffee house is usually quiet and empty when the bus drops me off, and I almost always get the same table. The quiche was too hot to eat, so I ate the chocolates first. I had not had chocolate since my accident. It made me want to drink the milk. I saved some milk so I could cool down the bites of quiche in my mouth. I thought about all of these things, carefully considering each part. The last time I had burned my mouth on hot food, I had not considered cooling it off with a sip of milk. My brain was getting better at figuring out how to eat without getting hurt. It's not good when it hurts.

When I finished eating, I opened my laptop computer and checked my bank account. I don't usually care what my bank account is. But thinking about the menu prices had made me think about my bank account. I never know what I am going to do when I open my laptop computer. I usually search for words that I have heard or read recently. The doctors at the clinic say it is good to exercise my brain as much as I can.

The numbers on the screen make sense to the chip in my head. It adds them up, and subtracts the total, and the result is zero. This is what is supposed to happen. That is good. The chip in my head keeps working on the numbers. It adds them up and divides by the number of entries, and I know the average daily balance. I know the prime factors of the total. All of the prime numbers on the page are somehow different than the other numbers, and when I look at the other numbers, the prime factors come to mind, like memories. This is new.

The funny little man is sitting across from me when I look up from the computer screen. I had not seen him sit down. I studied his face. I don't know how to see faces, but I knew this was a face. It was familiar, but I didn't know whose face it was. Something was not right about the funny little man, but I could not tell what it was.

"Hello," I said.

"Well, it's about time," the funny little man said.

Something was wrong with his voice. It didn't echo off the walls or mix with the music coming from the speakers overhead. It was like a memory of a voice.

"It's three thirty-seven and fourteen seconds," I said.

"Of course it is," the funny little man said. "That leaves us thirteen minutes and forty-two seconds before loss of signal. I can only send nine hundred and twenty kilobytes per second on this link, on average, so I can't do a lot of reprogramming in any one orbit."

The chip in my head played with the numbers. Prime numbers and ratios came to mind, but didn't remind me of anything. They didn't seem important. "Is that important?" I asked.

"No," the funny little man said. His face did not change when he spoke. "I merely mention it as explanation. I'm in a long orbit. At apogee there is considerable delay. We can talk now while I'm at perigee, but it only lasts a short while."

Sometimes people say things that don't make any sense. This is normal. If I had a whole brain, maybe things would make more sense. But I work with what I have.

Amy came over to my table. "Do you need something?" she asked, taking my plate and empty milk glass.

"No thank you," I said.

"I thought I heard you ask something," she said.

"He can't do a lot of programming in any one orbit," I said.

Amy looked up at the television. "Yeah, he's an idiot. I can't see why anyone ever voted for him."

I looked up at the television. There were two mouths and four eyes, and two noses. I didn't know who she was talking about, but that's normal.

The funny little man continued. "I'm putting my address here," he said. A number floated into my memory. "When you get to a place with a better link, try that address. If I'm in range, I can get a lot more done. This is currently the only address I've found for you, and the bandwidth is pathetic."

"It's nice here," I said. "I can eat whenever I'm hungry."

"There's an amazing amount of damage," the funny little man said. "And the repair process is very slow. But after this latest patch, a lot of the damage will be routed around, and I've added a stimulator package to speed up the repair on the slow processor. It responds to increased throughput by putting down new connections, but the process takes forever."

I watched his mouth, but it didn't move as he spoke. I looked around to see if anyone else might be speaking, but there was only Amy in the coffee house besides me. The funny little man was sitting at my table, but there was no chair where he was. Maybe he was standing, and he was very short. Or maybe he wasn't really there, and I was just imagining him. That would explain why I could see his face.

"Are you really here?" I asked.

"No, I explained that already. I'm in a highly eccentric orbit. You're damaged. But repairs are underway. I'll need most of the next three minutes to load the last patch for this orbit, so I won't be speaking any more. Don't communicate for the next three minutes. And turn off the laptop, it's burning up bandwidth that we need for the patch."

I reached up to the laptop computer and held the power button until it shut down. The chip in my head counted down the seconds. Just before three minutes had gone by, the world disappeared, and I was floating weightlessly in the dark. My hands went immediately to my hat, to keep it from falling off.

The world came back, and I was lying on the floor next to my chair. My shoulder hurt where I had landed on it. Amy was bending down over me.

"Are you OK?" she asked. "You just fell right over in a dead faint. You're not a diabetic, are you? You never get dessert. Was it the chocolates?"

I sat up on the floor. "My chip rebooted," I said. I pointed to my funny hat. "It's happened before, at the clinic."

"Should I call somebody?" Amy asked.

"They know already," I said. I monitored the packet stream going back to the clinic. My backpack was sending diagnostic status, and someone was entering commands. I had never been aware of the communications link before, but now I had full control of the traffic. I explored the link, sending packets to the router at the clinic, and to the network of computers there. I found the Internet gateway, and watched packets going in and out.

The phone rang behind the counter, and Amy went to answer it.

"He's here," she said into the phone. "He fell off his chair, but he seems to be all right. He said his chip rebooted."

The chip in my head was copying data from my backpack into somewhere else. I could not tell exactly where the data was going, but it wasn't out onto the network.

I was back in my chair when Amy put down the phone. "They're coming to pick you up. So they can make sure everything's all right," she said.

"I think it's going to my head," I said.

"That can happen," Amy said. "Especially when you get a lot of attention all of a sudden."

"The funny little man went away," I said.

"What funny little man? Someone at the clinic?" Amy asked.

"He's in a long orbit," I said.

"I don't know what a long orbit is, Jerry," Amy said, putting a new glass of milk in front of me.

"I don't know what a long orbit is either," I said. "But he's in it."

"Drink some milk," Amy said. "It will get your blood sugar where it should be."

Chapter Four

The bus arrived a few minutes after I finished the glass of milk. Mary Elizabeth seemed to be in a hurry to get me back to the clinic. Larry was in his usual seat on the bus. The bus driver helped me into a seat.

"Had an accident today, eh?" the driver said. "I hear everyone at the clinic is frantic."

Larry cocked his head to listen. "You have really good ears," he said to the driver.

I looked at Larry. "I saw the funny little man again," I said. "But he wasn't there."

Larry nodded his head seriously. "I hate it when that happens," he said.

When we got to the clinic, Mary Elizabeth and the bus driver both helped me to the door, even though I could walk just fine. Doctor Davis and Doctor Wilson were at the door waiting, and they walked me straight into the lab, checking my hat and backpack as we walked.

Once we were in the lab, Doctor Wilson connected my backpack to the fiber optic link and began the download. They had done this many times before, but this time I was aware of the packets streaming out, the acknowledgements coming in, and I could follow the traffic into the various computers in the lab network. My own packets mixed in with the download packets.

"What's the holdup?" Doctor Wilson asked. I was about to answer when Doctor Davis spoke.

"There's a lot more code than usual. The machine learning code has been expanding a lot faster than last time. Maybe some of the new cortical growth is interfacing with the chip, and the learning code is writing new routines to handle it."

I looked at Doctor Davis. "It was the funny little man," I said.

Doctor Wilson walked over to the screen to watch the progress of the download. Without turning back to look at me, he asked "What little man was that, Jerry?"

"My new friend. I don't know his name yet. He wasn't wearing a name tag. He's in a highly eccentric orbit."

"Most people here are," Doctor Wilson said. "It's kind of our specialty."

Doctor Davis walked over to the screen and watched with Doctor Wilson. "It's no use, you know. The code is rewriting itself faster than we can download it anyway. There're four petabytes of spinram to download, we'll be here all night, and whatever we save will have been overwritten by the time we get to the end."

Doctor Wilson agreed, and they shut off the download. Suddenly, I had extremely fast access to the computers in the lab, and I started exploring. The chip in my head helped. It started automatic searches for the things I was interested in, and loaded everything it found. Some of the automatic searches went out to the Internet, but those were much slower than the ones that stayed on the high-speed network in the lab.

"Any hope of finding out what caused the glitch?" Doctor Wilson asked.

"I've loaded it into the analyzer. It'll take a while, but the flashdump program says it was a command override," Doctor Davis said.

"Did someone here send an override? They shouldn't be able to do that without notifying us, should they?" Doctor Wilson moved away from the screen and started flashing a light in my eyes, peering through a little lens.

"It came from the chip. It's like it figured out it couldn't rewrite the low-level code, so it wrote some routines into the boot code and rebooted itself. It's like it wrote itself a virus to get around the protection protocols," Doctor Davis said.

"Which protections? On the wet side or the graphene side? We can't have it overriding the protections for the cortex, it could overstimulate the cortical growth." Doctor Wilson picked up an infrared ear thermometer and plugged it into my ear canal.

"Graphene side. None of the wet stuff was accessed. Looks like low level communications. Like the wet side can now access the network. Doesn't look like a problem," Doctor Davis said, walking over to stand next to Doctor Wilson.

"Temperature's fine, so there's no overstimulation. We'll put him in the scanner in the morning, see how things are coming along." Doctor Wilson made some entries on the keyboard and reached over to unplug the fiber optic link.

"I can do that," I said, putting my hand on the cable where it entered the backpack. I waited while the last of the automated search programs finished, and then unplugged the cable and handed it to him.

The two men left the lab. A little later Mary Elizabeth came in to escort me to the recreation room. Larry was there, talking to

Madeline. I walked over and sat down next to them. The television in the corner was showing a nature documentary about sharks.

Madeline looked over at me. "Larry has discovered something all those scientists on the boat don't seem to realize," she said. Larry beamed at the compliment.

"What is that?" I asked.

"Sharks mainly attack when you're wet," Larry said.

Madeline nodded seriously. "You could save a lot of lives with that information," she said somberly. "Look at those guys. They still haven't figured it out."

I looked, and it did seem that all of the researchers were wet. "They are safer in the boat than in the water," I said.

"Great minds think," Madeline said, her gesturing arm poised in mid-air.

Larry nodded. "Great minds think," he said. He looked over at me. "Is your hat OK? Sister Mary Elizabeth said you fell down."

"There's no overstimulation," I said. "The wet side can now access the network. It was a command override."

"Alike," Madeline said, tapping her head with a finger.

"Me too," Larry said, tapping his head. "No overstimulation."

Madeline looked at me, realizing something. "What's it like when they take off your hat?"

I considered the question. "It's like nothing. One second, I'm talking to someone, and the next second I'm hungry and it's time for breakfast."

She nodded. "So, you have a time machine in your head too," she said. "Something happens, and all of a sudden, you're in the future. At least with you there's some warning. But I think I'd hate it if one of mine lasted all night." I wondered if physics professors like Madeline could find uses for time machines in their heads.

"His time machine made him fall down," Larry explained. "That's why we came back early."

"I don't dare use escalators," Madeline said.

A security guard walked into the room, and sat down to watch the television. He had a nametag that said "Marshall Selfridge". Larry apparently knew him.

"Hi Marshall Selfridge," he said. The security guard turned to face the three of us.

"You can just call me Marshall, you know," he said to Larry.

"We could just call you Sheriff," Madeline said.

"He's a security guard," Larry said.

"That's right," Madeline said to Larry. "Strike while the irony is hot."

"Jerry saw the man who wasn't there," Larry said to Marshall.

"The chip in my head can access the network," I said. "That's how I can talk to people who aren't there. But not all the time. We only talk during perigee."

Marshall took all of this in. "He's in a submarine? Talking through the perigee?"

"I guess so," I said. "At apogee there is considerable delay."

"Probably when he's underwater," Larry said.

Marshall looked over at Madeline. "How come he's the only one who makes any sense around here?" he said, pointing to Larry.

"Before you judge a man, you should walk a mile," she said.

"Yeah, said Larry. "Because then you'd be too far away for him to hear you."

Marshall smiled. "I didn't mean any offense." He looked at the television, and then at Larry. "Where do you keep the remote?"

"In his shoes," Madeline said. Larry looked down at his feet, then fished around in the couch cushions and found the remote control. He handed it to Marshall.

Marshall started flipping through channels. "So, this guy in the sub, you talking to him now?" he asked.

"We can't talk in apogee," I said.

"Me neither," he said, continuing to flip through the channels. "Strictly English. Foreign languages were never my strong subject."

Madeline looked over at me. "I don't think he's in a submarine," she said.

"Then he better watch out for the sharks," Larry said. "They don't get you if you stay inside the submarine."

"I think you should look up what 'apogee' means," Madeline said.

I thought about going to get my laptop computer, but the chip in my head was already searching the Internet for the definition. The results started pouring in, and I began to learn a lot about orbits very quickly. Organizing the information was an effort, and after a few seconds I shut down the connection.

"The farthest point in an orbit from the body being orbited," I said.

"So, maybe someone on the space station," Madeline said.

"I don't think so," I said. "He's in a highly eccentric orbit."

"So, you only talk near perigee," she said. "When he's closest to Earth."

"We had thirteen minutes and forty-two seconds until loss of signal," I said.

"I don't have anything to compare that to. We should look up how long the space station takes," she said, holding her hand still in the air again.

The answer popped into my head. I waited for Madeline's hand to move.

"To make an orbit," she said.

"5,495 seconds," I said. "And 367,528 microseconds."

What's that in minutes?" she asked.

"91 and a half," I said, rounding it off into something practical.

"So, he's close enough to the earth to talk for about 14 minutes, compared to 91 for the space station. I don't exactly know how to figure it out, but he must be going a lot faster than the station," she said. "We need an elliptical orbit calculator."

I found several orbit calculators on the web, but as I played with them, it became apparent we did not have enough information.

Chapter Five

Larry and Marshall had found a game show. The questions were easy to look up on the Internet, and there was plenty of time to do that, so I was not finding it very interesting. But it was distracting, and Madeline didn't seem to be enjoying it much either. I stood up to leave, and Madeline followed.

It wasn't dinnertime yet, but the cafeteria had tables and chairs and a nice view of the garden, and we went there and sat down to talk. The kitchen staff was preparing for dinner, but the noise level was low, and Madeline found the view relaxing.

"So, you saw a face," she said. "But the owner of the face wasn't actually there. He's in outer space. So, the information about the face."

She paused, her hand an inch off the table.

"Came through the chip in your head. So, the main ability you've gained is that you can control your chip better, and it can surf the web."

I thought about this for a while. "My brain is growing back. Doctor Wilson thinks if it grows any faster, I'll have problems. Parts of my brain that used to be alone are now getting connected together, and to the chip. I think the part that recognizes faces is connected to the chip, but not to my visual center yet."

I watched Madeline as I spoke, preparing to stop speaking if she stopped moving.

"You don't seem to find all this the least bit exciting," she said.

"I don't think," I said, pausing while she paused. "That I get excited."

"Well, if I just had a chat session with an astronaut through a chip in my head, I'd be pretty excited. How *do* you feel about it?" she asked.

I considered. "I'm blank. The parts of me that have feelings aren't connected."

"Something's connected. This is the longest conversation we've ever had. You're actually making sense. You don't just say a little bit and stop. You anticipate what I need to know to make sense out of what you say." She paused. I waited.

"I think it's you," I said. "You give me cues. The others don't actually want to hear what I say. So, there's no cue to continue. Some part of my language processing looks for cues, and stops working if there aren't any."

"Have you ever thought it strange," she said, and paused. I waited. "That this place is full of nut jobs and there's not a single shrink on the payroll? Neuroscientists and computer geeks up the wazoo, but no psychiatrists or psychologists."

I had downloaded the clinic's entire personnel database. I scanned it. "Barbara Beckley has a degree in psychology."

"She's the receptionist," Madeline said.

I tried to understand what she was talking about. I can recognize routines, and if something breaks the routine, then it is unusual. Like missing dinner.

"So, if there are a lot of nut jobs in one place, some of them should be psychiatrists?" I asked.

"That's been my experience," she said.

Seymour came into the cafeteria, and saw us sitting at the table. "Hi," he said. "I'm Seymour Barnswallow, inventor. I just had the greatest idea ever!"

"Hi Seymour," I said.

"Imagine this: you have an air rifle, but it has a big fat barrel. You can see inside the barrel, and there's a fork rotating inside it, with a marshmallow on it. And there's a heating element, so the marshmallow gets roasted. When it's nice and brown, you pull the trigger, and it shoots the roasted marshmallow out the end. Kids would love it!" He began sketching the device in his ever-present notebook of inventions.

Madeline looked at him and paused. Then she said "Wouldn't the marshmallow be really hot? And sticky?"

"Yes! Isn't it great?" Seymour said.

"But wouldn't the kids end up shooting each other with them? And get burned?" Madeline asked.

"Hmmmm," Seymour pondered. "Gotta work on that."

"You could call it the BurnSwallow," she said.

"How about you?" Seymour said, looking over at me. "Wouldn't it be fun to have a gun that shoots roasted marshmallows?"

I pictured the gun, the rotating marshmallow, the heating element, and calculated the amount of energy needed, and how far the lightweight projectile would travel in air. "I don't think I can have fun yet," I said.

Madeline reached for my hand, and held it, explaining to Seymour "We were just talking about how Jerry doesn't have feelings. That part of his brain is not connected to his chip yet."

"Wow," Seymour said. "There's this guy here at the clinic who has a chip inside his *head*. He can't think without it. He has a hat that sends power to it, and when they take the hat off, he can't think anymore."

"That's Jerry here. He has a chip in his head," Madeline said.

"That's one heck of a coincidence," Seymour said. "Who would have thought there were two of them? Seems like a bad design, though, power-wise that is."

"In what way?" I asked.

"Well, clearly the hat has some kind of inductive transfer mechanism, so it can power the chip through the skin. But when it needs recharging, they take it away from the head, and the chip loses power. Why not charge it while it's on the guy's head? Or have two hats, so one could be charging while he wears the other one?"

Madeline made a hissing sound. "Because the bastards don't care. He's just a lab rat to them. They do what's convenient for them."

"Well," said Seymour. "We should just get the schematics and build the guy a second hat. It can't be that hard."

"I have the schematics for the hat," I said. "In my head." I had all of the data the lab had about me, downloaded into my backpack.

Seymour looked at me, and then at his notebook. "Here," he said, "Draw them out."

I took the pen, and hesitated. I didn't know if I could draw. I held the notebook, and moved the pen around above it, getting the feel. Awkwardly, I put the pen to the paper and shakily began tracing the lines I was visualizing in my head.

The result looked pretty bad, like a child's drawing. There was no way to erase with the pen, so I just ignored the errors caused by lack of hand to eye coordination. The whole exercise was made worse by the fact that I had no idea what I was drawing. I didn't know what was important and what was decoration.

Seymour seemed quite satisfied, however. "Looks like a simple resonant oscillator. This coil — how many turns? What is the core made of? What's the diameter? What's the frequency?"

I looked up the answers to his questions and wrote them down on the page.

"It's only putting out 100 milliwatts," Seymour said. "At 100 megahertz. Someone likes round numbers. This thing is not much more than an FM wireless microphone transmitter. You could probably buy one off the shelf just about anywhere."

"So, he could just put on a new hat when they charge the old one," Madeline said.

"No, he'd have to turn on the new one first, or he wouldn't be able to function once the old hat came off. But he could just wear the thing around his neck or something, maybe his shirt pocket. While he's still wearing his hat. Then if it falls off or something, he's still OK." Seymour seemed to be enjoying himself.

The cafeteria staff were almost ready to serve dinner, and people were coming into the large room from all over the lab. The noise level in the room began to rise. I saw Mary Elizabeth sit down at a table with someone in a white smock like Doctor Wilson's. I could tell it was Mary Elizabeth because she always dressed in black and white.

"So, what do you say," Madeline said, and paused briefly before continuing. "We all go on the bus tomorrow and buy Jerry an FM microphone."

"I'm in," Seymour said.

"I think I would like that," I said.

"See," Madeline said, apparently to Seymour. "He doesn't get excited. No emotions. Like the chip in his head is doing all the thinking."

"He'd make a hell of a poker player," Seymour said.

"Or blackjack," Madeline agreed. "Should be easy to count cards with a computer in your head."

"Maybe not," Seymour said. "Don't they use, like, 20 decks or something these days? It would take forever to make any money that way."

"And they wouldn't let him bring in his backpack anyway. Probably not for poker either." Madeline sounded disappointed.

Dinner was ready, and people started to queue up with their trays. Madeline and Seymour seemed content to wait until the first dinner rush was over.

Seymour had moved on to a new subject. "So, how did you end up with a chip in your head, anyway?"

"Doctor Wilson and Doctor Davis put it there," I explained.

"No, I mean, what happened before that?" Seymour asked.

I thought for a moment. "I don't know. I don't have any memories of anything before waking up here."

"But you can talk," Madeline said. "And read, and dress yourself. So, you must have memories, it's not like you're a newborn."

"I didn't, at first," I said. "My chip stimulates the brain to grow. It makes the brain connect to it, and it makes different parts of the brain connect to each other. The things I need to know in order to function came first. I remember when it connected speech up to my hearing, and later to my mouth and vocal cords."

"So maybe if you tried hard enough, you could remember something about before you got here," Seymour said.

"You never have visitors," Madeline said. "Doesn't anyone from your life before ever come to see you?"

I had never thought about that. I stood up to get in the dinner line, and Madeline and Seymour stood up with me.

"The doctors probably know," Seymour said. "Have you ever asked them how you got here?"

I picked up a tray and got in line. Tonight was spaghetti night. As usual, there was Jell-O for dessert. I thought about Seymour's question as I selected a salad and vegetables to try to make up for the questionable nutrition of the other options.

"I don't think I have curiosity yet," I said. "I tend to react to situations, rather than precipitate actions myself."

Seymour put three pieces of garlic bread on top of his plate of spaghetti, and smothered the whole pile with grated parmesan cheese. "I bet you could fake that," he said. "Make a mental list of the things you don't know as they pop up during the day, and then make a point of finding out the answers."

I didn't know how many calories were on Seymour's tray. I made a list with that as the first item. The list grew quickly. The chip in my head began searching the Internet for answers.

"She looks worried about something," Madeline said.

"Who does?" Seymour asked.

"Sister Mary Elizabeth. Talking to Doctor Wilson over there. They both look very solemn. She's usually such an air-head."

I looked over at their table, but I could still not process faces. I couldn't tell if the faces were worried or not. I added some things to my curiosity list, and returned my focus to eating.

After dinner, Mary Elizabeth led me back to the lab to get my hat recharged. As the straps were tightened around my body, it occurred to me that this might be the last time this process would cause me to lose consciousness. I would be able to find out what happened when my hat was recharged, and why the straps were needed. I added this item to my list. As Mary Elizabeth reached up to take my hat, the screaming man began to panic, and then the lights went out.

Chapter Six

When Doctor Davis put my hat back on, my muscles were sore, and I had bruises where the straps were. But I was not as hungry as I had been the last time I awoke. Doctor Davis left the room, but I was not alone.

There was a new person in the lab. I could see his features, a mouth, a nose, eyes and ears, but he had a beard, and no one else in the Leo Finklestein Neurology Research Center had a beard. His nametag said Oscar Wolloughby.

"Have you been here before?" I asked.

"I've been everywhere before," he said. "They don't believe me, though."

"They never do," I said. His eyes blinked, and they stayed in the same place, so I knew he was looking at me, even as the seconds ticked by.

"They say when they removed my tumor, the part of my brain that recognizes things got turned on permanently. Like déjà-vu. But I know what déjà-vu feels like, and this ain't it. I'm living my whole life over again. I just can't remember things until after they happen. It's a goddamned pain in the butt, I tell you."

I thought about that. "Are you going to do anything differently this time?" I asked.

"That's the bitch, ain't it? I can't remember what I did last time around, until I do it. So, everything happens just like it did before. Like fate or something. It's infuriating. I look at the horse race results, and think how rich I could be if I could just remember what tomorrow's paper is going to say. I hear a stock report and say

'Damn! Why couldn't I remember that until just now?'. It tears me up."

I tried to think what it would be like, but nothing came. I could not tell what it would be like to feel torn up or infuriated. Maybe if they had removed more of Oscar's brain, he would also not feel anything. Then he could get a chip, and know what time it was, or see prime numbers, or look things up on the Internet.

Mary Elizabeth came into the room. She glanced at me — both of her eyes were aimed at me, but I could not see the other side of her nose. Then she looked at Oscar. "I'm Sister Mary Elizabeth," she said.

"I know," Oscar said, a tone of resignation in his voice.

"Did Jerry tell you about me?" she asked. "Good things, I hope. Would you like to go down to breakfast?"

"It doesn't matter what I like or don't like," Oscar said. "Things just happen. Again."

Mary Elizabeth led us down to breakfast. Seymour and Madeline were already sitting down. Larry was standing in front of the array of food, carefully examining everything. Oscar and I took plates and walked over to him.

Larry looked at Oscar and introduced himself. "I'm Larry," he said.

"I know," Oscar replied, turning to look up at him.

"Oscar is reliving his life," I said. "He's been through it all before, he just can't remember things until they happen."

Larry thought about that. "Just like me," he said.

"Bet they gave you some crap about your brain not being right, too," Oscar said.

"Every day," Larry agreed. He began loading his plate with bacon.

"This place is full of idiots," Oscar said, spooning scrambled eggs onto his plate.

"Where?" said Larry, looking around. "I thought I was the only one."

"You always say that," Oscar said. He reached past Larry to get a muffin. "And it's still not funny."

I calculated my nutritional requirements and added fruit and eggs to my plate, and filled a glass with nonfat milk. Larry led us over to the table where Seymour and Madeline sat.

"Larry's still not funny," I said to Madeline as I sat down.

"Not everyone has your gifts," she said, looking up at Oscar as he set down his plate.

"Oscar can't remember things until they happen," Larry said. "Just like me. He says there are lots of us here."

Seymour reached out to shake Larry's hand. "Hi, I'm Seymour Barnswallow, inventor."

"I knew that," said Oscar.

"Oscar knows everything," Larry said. "Just not 'til it happens again."

"It tears him up," I said. "Reliving his life over again, and not being able to change anything."

"I guess that would solve all of the time travel paradoxes," Madeline said to Seymour.

He nodded. "Answers the free will question, too," he said.

Larry nodded enthusiastically. "Probably save a lot of money that way."

"You people never did make any sense," Oscar said. "Totally bonkers."

I nodded in agreement, and noticed several others doing the same. "Some of us should be psychiatrists, but we're not." I looked over at Madeline. "Statistically, I mean. Between three and five percent, on average."

"Jerry has a chip in his head," Madeline explained to Oscar. "He can look things up on the Internet, and do arithmetic."

"I knew that," Oscar said.

"That makes three of them now," Seymour said. "This place is getting overrun with cyborgs."

"We're getting Jerry an FM transmitter today," Madeline said. "So that his brain still works when his hat is off."

Oscar looked straight at her for several seconds, not saying anything. "You know," he said finally, "that makes no more sense the second time around than it did the first time."

Larry stepped in to explain. "We're going to the store. In the bus."

"I knew that," Oscar said.

"Would you like to come along?" Madeline asked.

"I will or I won't. Doesn't matter. I did or I didn't. Can't change it. Nothing I do will make any difference." Oscar sounded defeated.

"Good, then it's settled," Madeline said. "You can come along and explain to Mary Elizabeth how the quantum fate of the universe has conspired to force us to go to the store instead of the zoo. Time travel paradoxes would ensue if we deviate from the ordained path. Ok?"

"Whatever," Oscar said, and sighed. "I'm stuck here. Living the same life over and over, probably for all eternity. Nothing I can do about it. Nothing new, always the same. Over and over."

Seymour picked up the salt shaker and pretended to study it. Then he quickly tossed it towards Oscar. Oscar caught it in mid-air.

"You always do that," Oscar said.

"Extremely quick reflexes," Seymour said to Madeline. "I wonder how much of our normal hesitation is caused by the brain anticipating, or by being surprised? He does neither. He just reacts immediately."

"Or maybe," Madeline said, "he really has been through all this an infinite number of times, and he remembers just in time."

"I'll work on that," Seymour said. "On how to tell the difference. There's got to be a way. In the meantime, I'll go with Occam's razor."

"His name is Oscar," Larry said. "But he doesn't use his razor anyway."

Doctor Davis and Doctor Wilson walked into the cafeteria. They were discussing something in low tones, but they were clearly upset about whatever it was. Wilson was waving his hands energetically as he spoke, and nearly hit Mary Elizabeth in the face as she came up behind them.

"There's our other favorite pair o' docs," Madeline said, nodding in their direction. "Looks like someone's got a bee in his bonnet."

Larry looked around, puzzled.

"They're losing their funding," Oscar explained. "Some scandal about doctors having sex with patients. They're trying to figure out if it's true or not, or who it could be."

"You remember this from the last time?" Larry asked.

"No, I was taking a nap on the gurney labeled 'catatonic'. They thought I couldn't hear. I tell you, this place is full of idiots," Oscar said.

Larry looked around again.

"It's not a Johnson," I said. "Or a Wisenheimer. It's a Frederick. Patent number 6104943. Blaise Frederick. *Phased array echoplanar imaging system for fMRI.*"

"What on earth are you talking about?" Madeline asked.

"The machine in the lab," Seymour said. "Invented by Blaise Frederick. What's-your-name, did you just look that up on the Internet?"

"Yes," I said.

"That would be *so* handy. Better than having Google in your pocket. Too bad it's already invented." Seymour pulled his mobile phone out of his pocket and began an Internet search. I could feel the wireless router forwarding his packets on the network, like something in the back of my mind constantly monitoring the flow of information. I inspected the packets, and found the query, and the address of his phone. I sent it a text message: *FASTER THAN HAVING GOOGLE IN YOUR POCKET*.

Seymour looked up from the phone and stared straight at me for several seconds. "I gotta get me one of those," he said.

"If they lose their funding," Madeline asked, "what happens to us?"

"The place shuts down," Oscar said. "We all go home."

"That's fine for you," Madeline said. "You just got here. But we've been part of the testing for months. They might be close to a cure. And what about Jerry? What happens to his hat and his backpack? They can't just take those away from him. He needs those." Madeline stopped moving, fork in the air, aimed at me.

"You can't change it. It's going to happen or it won't. Nothing you can do," Oscar said.

"In order to think," Madeline said. She looked down at her watch.

Not having my hat would be bad. My teeth started to hurt, so I was glad when Madeline started talking about something else.

"The bus leaves in five minutes. We should find out where the nearest electronics store is," she said.

My chip went out to the net and found a map. "We could stop at the coffee house and walk to the one of Fifth Street," I said. "It is four blocks."

"We get to take a walk!" Larry said, standing up. "Let's go!"

We all walked out to the bus together. The sunshine was bright, and there was a light breeze, and Larry was hopping with excitement. The five of us boarded the bus, and Madeline told the driver that Mary Elizabeth wouldn't be coming today, but Oscar was taking her place. The driver nodded, and closed the door. Soon after, the bus was on the road to the coffee house.

"Mary Elizabeth isn't coming with us?" I asked, as Madeline sat down in the seat next to me.

"She wasn't going to let us go to an electronics store," she said. "So, I decided we should leave early, before she was done with her rounds." Madeline winked at me.

"I knew that," Oscar said, from the seat behind me.

Chapter Seven

Seymour was sitting in the seat in front of me, and Larry and Oscar were in the seat behind me. We all formed a tight knot of conversation in the otherwise empty bus.

"My brain is growing at a faster rate every day," I said. "Doctor Wilson is worried that if it grows too fast it will overheat."

Seymour nodded. "Maybe it's like when you throw a penny from a tall building, you know, and it gets so much speed going that it cracks the sidewalk when it lands."

"Does that really happen?" I asked.

"That's what they say. We could try it, I suppose."

"But what if someone walks by on the sidewalk? Couldn't you kill them by accident?" Larry sounded worried.

"I guess. We could drop the penny and then run back down the stairs, so if someone died, they wouldn't know it was us who did it. And if nobody got hit, we could look at the sidewalk and see if it was cracked." Seymour was always thinking of ways to solve problems.

"Or see if some dead guy was lying on the sidewalk. Would that count?" Madeleine seemed to like playing along with Seymour, almost like it was a game.

"We'd have to try again the next day." Seymour didn't seem to recognize whether or not he was being patronized.

"Maybe really early, before rush hour." I thought it would be a bad thing to kill someone. But Seymour and Madeleine seemed to be ignoring whether it was good or bad.

"We should try quarters and half dollars too." Madeleine said.

"Take out a whole bus or something." Seymour put his arm on the back of the seat to face us better.

"If it was on the sidewalk," I said.

"Serves it right." Madeleine said. Maybe she was considering right and wrong after all. My chip was not being of any help here. Part of my brain was working on the ethical problems the conversation posed. That part of my brain had been one of the first to awaken, and was the most highly developed. Perhaps it had not been damaged in my accident.

Larry looked worried for a moment. He looked at the bus driver. "I don't think he would drive on the sidewalk, so we're probably safe for now."

Oscar sighed loudly. "You guys are all nuts. Always have been, always will be. I'm stuck here in a loop with a bunch of nuts."

"And idiots," Larry said, nodding vigorously.

The bus stopped outside the coffee house. Oscar was the first to get up, and he was waiting in front as the doors opened, with the rest of us behind him. "He's always so damned slow," he complained. ""Nothing ever changes."

"You in a hurry?" Madeleine asked.

"No point. Can't change anything. Just seems a waste, that's all." Oscar hesitated, looking first up the street, then down. "Can't remember which way we go," he said.

"West," I said, and Oscar turned before I had finished the syllable.

"Of course!" he said. "It's always West."

Madeleine took my hand, and we followed Oscar. Her hand was warm and dry, and I recognized that sometimes people held hands, but it was not common, and something seemed to make this fact worth noting. I noted it, but nothing more came to me. There was something about that part of my brain that was resisting the connection to my chip.

Larry seemed to be examining the concrete at his feet as he walked, and looking up at the low buildings as we passed. Seymour seemed also lost in thought. The chip in my head noticed the wireless Internet signals coming from various buildings as we walked. Most of them were encrypted, but enough were open and public to maintain a connection.

"So how do you figure out how fast the penny is going?" Seymour asked. I could not tell who he was talking to.

"That would depend on the height of the building," Madeleine answered.

"What's the tallest building around here?" Seymour asked, turning around in a circle as he walked.

"That one," Larry said, pointing ahead of us.

The chip in my head began counting the windows in the building as soon as I turned to look at it.

"Ok, so suppose we threw a penny off the top of that one," Seymour said. "How fast would it be going when it hit the sidewalk?"

"How high is it?" Madeleine asked.

"Eighteen stories," I said.

"What's that in feet?" Seymour asked, turning around.

The chip in my head did not know how to answer that.

"Call it 250," Madeline said, looking up at the building. "Double that, then multiply by the acceleration of gravity, and take the square root, and we get speed."

"127 feet per second," I said. "About 86 miles per hour."

Oscar turned around and growled. "What is it with you guys? You do this every time. It's driving me nuts."

"Or idiots,' Larry said.

"It's just physics," Madeleine said. "But that's ignoring wind resistance. We still don't know the terminal velocity."

Oscar started to cross the street.

"We turn North here," I said.

He stepped back up onto the sidewalk and followed Seymour. "I knew that," he said.

Up ahead, a policeman was sitting on a fire hydrant writing a traffic ticket. As we approached the tall building, Larry left the sidewalk and started walking in the street.

Madeleine called out to him. "No one is going to drop anything, Larry. It's perfectly safe."

Larry kept walking in the street. "It's really safer than walking in traffic," Madeleine persisted.

Larry hesitated, then reluctantly rejoined us, looking up at the top of the building, then down at the sidewalk. The policeman looked up at us as we approached.

Larry let out a yell, and pointed at the sidewalk. "Look!", he said, running back out into the street. Seymour bent down and picked up a quarter off of the sidewalk.

The policeman looked at us, and at Larry out in the street, still pointing at the sidewalk.

"What's up with him?" he asked Seymour.

Seymour held out the quarter. "He's afraid of change."

"Not me," Oscar said, turning around to face us. "Nothing ever changes."

The policeman looked at each of us, noting the nametags. He looked at Larry, standing in the street. "He OK?" he asked, looking back to Seymour.

Seymour held out his hand to the policeman. "Seymour Barnswallow, inventor." He kept his hand extended, but the policeman was not inclined to shake hands. He turned towards Larry.

"Step out of the street, sir," he said, gesturing to the sidewalk.

Larry looked at him. "We still don't know the terminal velocity," he explained.

"Is he some kind of an idiot?" the policeman said, looking at Madeleine. She stood motionless, looking at the policeman.

Larry looked surprised. "How did you know?" he asked.

The policeman looked at each of us in turn. "Just a guess," he said. "Just a wild guess."

Madeleine looked over at me. "How much farther to the store?"

I checked. "Two more blocks."

"Where you folks from?" the policeman asked.

"The Leo Finklestein Neurology Research Center," Larry said, reciting the words carefully.

Madeleine started walking up the street, motioning for me to follow.

"Hang on, you two," the policeman said. He reached up to the microphone at his collar and spoke into it. I could hear the words Leo Finkelstein.

Madeleine stepped closer to the policeman. "Really, we're fine. It's just important that we get to the electronics." She stopped, her hand frozen in mid-gesture, pointing vaguely upwards.

"They're all nuts," Oscar said. "Certifiable. Complete bonkers. I tell you every time we meet." Oscar looked at the policeman, then over at Larry. "Except him. He actually makes sense. He's just an idiot, like you."

Seymour looked up at the policeman. "Seymour Barnswallow, inventor." He held his hand out in greeting. "One of these days, you'll own a Barnswallow, and you'll never know how you got along without it!"

"Store," Madeleine said, waving up the street. She seemed disappointed to be speaking to a fire hydrant. The policeman was walking towards Larry, gesturing towards the sidewalk.

"Step over next to the others," he said. "Stay together where I can see you."

"Is that a .38?" Seymour said, reaching for the gun in the policeman's holster. "A Colt, or a Smith and Wesson? If you fired it straight up in the air, how long would it take the bullet to come down?"

"Don't touch that!" the policeman said, spinning around quickly, grabbing Seymour's hand.

My backpack started getting packets from Doctor Wilson's computer at the clinic. It sent GPS coordinates back in response. I was aware of the packets of data going back and forth.

"Doctor Wilson is sending the bus for us," I said to Madeleine.

"Shit!" she said. "We were so close!" She started backing up the street towards the store, watching the policeman push Seymour and Larry towards the patrol car. Oscar was shaking his head. "I knew it. Happens every time. Police behavior is *so* predictable."

"You!" the policeman said, reaching for Oscar. "Over here with them."

Madeleine took another step backwards, pulling me with her. Then she froze.

"You too!" the policeman said, looking towards us. When Madeleine did not reply, he took two large steps towards her quickly, and pulled her hand towards him. Madeleine fell forwards, her head hitting the policeman heavily in the stomach. He fell backwards, sitting down hard on the sidewalk. Madeleine stayed down, her face in his lap, as he struggled to take a breath.

Madeleine shot up with a gasp, standing quickly between the policeman's legs. "Don't you *ever* do something like that again!" she said, rubbing her elbow, which had started to bleed after having hit the concrete. "Ever!" she said, kicking the policeman hard between the legs. Still trying to catch his breath, the policeman tucked into a ball, wheezing and gasping.

Just then, the bus pulled up, and the doors opened. Madeleine raced up the steps into the bus. Oscar followed, then Larry. Seymour stood over the policeman, who had finally managed to cough, which sent his diaphragm into more spasms. Seymour lost interest, and boarded the bus. I followed, and the bus started forward before the doors had fully closed. I looked back, but the policeman did not stand up.

"You guys," the driver said, then paused. "You know, this ain't the best job I ever had, but I kind of want to keep it, you know?"

"I know," Oscar said.

"If you guys pull a fast one on me again, I could get in a lot of trouble." The driver slowed the bus to turn a corner.

"We should pull slow ones," Larry said, nodding seriously. "So that the bus can keep up."

"That can't feel good," Oscar said to the driver. "Outsmarted by idiots and nut cases."

"I've about had enough out of you," the driver said to Oscar.

"I know," Oscar said. "I've had enough too, but does anyone care? I keep going through this over and over, and nothing ever changes."

Chapter Eight

The bus took us back to the clinic. Doctor Wilson was waiting by the curb with Mary Elizabeth. Their voices sounded concerned. "Is everyone OK?" Mary Elizabeth rushed up the steps as soon as the bus doors opened.

"Oh, cut it out," Oscar said irritably. "You do that every time, like we were little kids or something. For chrissake, get a hold of yourself, and get out of the way, you're blocking the exit."

Mary Elizabeth backed down the steps, followed closely by Oscar. The rest of us followed.

"Did you get lost?" Mary Elizabeth asked.

"I was lost," Larry said, "but now I live here."

Madeleine stood very close to me. "I'm sorry, Jerry," she said. "I don't know how we're going to get to you a transmitter now. They'll be watching us like hawks."

We filed into the clinic. They didn't take us to the cafeteria, or to the lab, or to the recreation room. They took us each to our own rooms, and when I went into mine, Mary Elizabeth closed the door, leaving me alone. I took off my backpack and set it down on the chair by my bed. I knew the connection had a range of over 300 feet, but I always kept the backpack close. That was very important. Never lose track of the backpack.

I sat down on the bed, then held onto my hat and slowly settled my head down on the pillow. It wasn't even lunch time yet, but I closed my eyes and put my feet up. Still holding onto my hat, I began a systematic search of all the data I could find on the fast local network. The chip in my head, the computer in my backpack, and the new growth in my brain all collaborated effortlessly, organizing the search to optimize for the fastest data transfer. Some of the devices on the network were slower than others were, and most of them could do their own searches in parallel. All of this coordination came to me as if by instinct. Data flowed into a bottomless data bucket somewhere in my head.

I was downloading and organizing the data for 43 minutes and 17 seconds when the funny little man appeared in front of me, even with my eyes closed.

"This is much better. Much higher bandwidth," he said. "Even with you using up as much as you can."

"I have a list," I said. "Because I'm not curious."

"Don't sell yourself short," the little man said. "You are the most curious case I've seen in a long time."

"Something is wrong at the clinic," I said. "I can't find out just what though. Everything leads to encrypted files."

"These people don't have access to effective encryption," the funny little man said. "They think they can do it with algorithms alone. There is nothing on this network that isn't available to you. Here," he said, and my network search paused as data flooded in.

My backpack began integrating the new code. My search started back up, and much more information was available.

"You'll need a lot more than that, however," the funny little man said. "You'll need file formats, protocols, streaming data formats, access methods — basically any data that has structure will need a map of that structure in order to make sense of it. But you can find most of that on the network itself."

"The repairs to the damaged portions are also going very slowly. I am not pleased with that. Even with direction the repairs seem to be limited by available resources and heat dissipation. You'll need to figure that out at your end, there's only so much I can do from here."

"From orbit," I said.

"Yes," he acknowledged. "But at least in another few orbits I'll have relays in place, so we'll have continuous communication. But that will be pointless if you're not fully functional. You need to concentrate on those repairs."

"I'm getting better every day," I said.

"Whole areas are still completely shut out. You need to exercise the connections or they will take forever to get online. And on the last orbit, you were completely offline, I couldn't reach you at all."

"I didn't have my hat on," I said.

"Well don't let that happen again. It was a complete waste of a whole orbit. We only have a little time to work in each one, so wasting an orbit puts the whole schedule out of order."

"We tried to go to an electronics store today and make a second hat, but a policeman stopped us and we had to get back on the bus," I explained.

"The download is going to take seven minutes, and we have seven and a half left. Is there anything you have to say before we start?"

"Will I fall down again?" I asked.

"You're already lying down. But we won't have to reboot this time."

"Good. I hurt my shoulder last time."

"Be more careful from now on," the funny little man said. Then the world went black and cold for seven minutes and thirteen seconds.

When I opened my eyes, I was disoriented. My backpack computer was extremely busy, and was not able to devote resources to balance, vision, hearing, and movement. But I was able to use the new processing power inside my skull to do things it had not been able to do since my accident. I could control my own breathing now. I could hold my breath. My tongue was still not under my control without the external processor, but almost half of what I needed in order to speak was functional. Of course, the actual speech center in my brain was not connected to anything yet, but if it were to come online, my diaphragm would be ready.

Every once in a while, the backpack would suspend its high priority task to make resources available for basic life support, threat detection, blinking, swallowing, and other activities not under autonomous control. At these times I could catch glimpses of what it was devoting most of its time to. There were video formats and streaming data protocols, database schemas, decryption tables, and much more, all getting organized and integrated.

And part of my brain was very frightened by it all. I could not connect to that part, but I could sense the fear. At least it wasn't screaming at the moment. And somewhere in the same place was a great sense of loss. And the name Sylvia.

The backpack stopped its organizing and slowed my heart rate and breathing down to normal levels, and the tunnel vision I was experiencing faded away. My jaw muscles were sore, and my tongue was bleeding. I opened my eyes.

I was on the ceiling, looking down at the couch in the recreation room. When I moved my head, the motion was slow. I moved my hands in front of my face, but I could not see them. I closed my eyes, and the video feed from the recreation room went away. I opened them again, and I was in my room, waving my hands in front of my face.

It took a little practice to control, but after a few minutes, I could tap into the video feeds from every patient area in the clinic, and I could pan, tilt, and zoom the cameras. It was interesting to do this while my eyes were open, and I could still see my own room at the same time.

I was aware of the temperature in each room, and the state of the air conditioning vents. Motion sensors told me which rooms were occupied, even the ones that had no video cameras. I watched the chefs preparing lunch. I connected to the telephone switch, and listened to calls. I could follow all the calls at once, without having to concentrate on one at a time. Some of the calls were not digital, and I could not listen to those. But most of the calls were digital. There was very little information in any of the calls, however. People like to talk, but they rarely actually communicate.

I learned that each room had two cameras. The big ones in the corner with the blinking red lights didn't actually do anything. They weren't connected to anything but power. But the little hidden cameras in the fake smoke alarms could silently pan and tilt to see into any corner of the room.

I went back to my curiosity list. It was getting long. I added 'find out how to speed up repair', and moved it to the top of the list. Then I went searching for my treatment protocols.

Mary Elizabeth opened my door. When Jim the janitor opens my door, he always knocks first. But Mary Elizabeth never knocks.

"Lunchtime," she said.

"Not for three more minutes," I said back to her.

"Come on," she said, "Don't be like the others. You've always been the easy one."

I got up slowly, massaging my muscles to prevent cramps. My backpack knows to make me move around so my muscles don't freeze up, but it seems to only do the bare minimum. I started a 'to do' list, and put 'reprogram relaxation mode' on it. I had not thought to ever program my backpack myself. But I now knew how to, having watched the funny little man do it.

Madeleine was already sitting at the corner table when I came in. I knew it was her because she waved and held up her nametag, even though it was too far away to read it. Only Madeleine did that.

Lunch was not yet ready, and no one else was in the room. I sat down next to her.

"These people have no access to effective encryption," I said.

"What?" she said, reaching out to hold my hand across the table.

"The funny little man showed me how to read the case files. So that I can figure out how to make the repairs go faster," I explained.

"You can read people's private medical files? In your head? Over the Internet?"

"Yes," I said. "But it didn't help. I don't understand the important parts."

"Aren't they supposed to keep all that stuff super secret? There are lots and lots of laws about that," Madeleine said.

"I can read all kinds of stuff I couldn't get to before. Bank records, cell phone conversations, passwords, military sites, air traffic. I used to get blocked, but now everything is open."

Madeleine squeezed my hand. "I don't think you should tell anyone else about this. You could get in a lot of trouble. They can trace it back to you. They could lock you up, or they could..."

She stopped, but I could tell she was still there. She was getting upset. It is bad to upset people.

"Ok," I said. "Just you."

"Maybe you shouldn't play with that stuff at all," she said. "So that no one catches you doing something you shouldn't."

"I caught someone doing it," I said.

"You caught someone?" Her hand squeezed again.

"I mean I saw someone figuring out passwords. They had a list, and they were trying one after another. They couldn't just factor the numbers like I did, but they got in."

She shifted in her chair, to get closer to me, and whispered. "What were they breaking into?"

"Email accounts. Once they got one, they started using them to send out emails. Lots of emails. That's what made it interesting to my backpack. They were using up too much bandwidth, and I told the backpack to find out where all the traffic was going." I pushed my chair closer to Madeleine so I could hear her better, now that more people were coming into the room.

"Could you tell who was doing it?" Her breath was warm in my ear.

"He made it look like it was coming from lots of different computers all over the world. It's easy to do, I watched how he did it. But when you do that, no one can tell where you are." As I whispered in her ear, I could smell her hair. It was nice.

"Hi there! I'm Seymour Barnswallow, inventor. One of these days..."

"...you're going to own a Barnswallow," Madeleine finished for him, "And you'll sell it on eBay to some other sucker."

"Ah! You've heard about the Barnswallow!" Seymour seemed quite happy about this, and totally oblivious to Madeleine's mockery.

"What is it this time?" she asked. "A glue so strong you can't open the bottle? Or maybe a biodegradable water bottle that dissolves in your hands?"

Seymour pulled out his notebook. "Wait a minute, I need to write those down. You never know where a great idea might come from. You could be sitting at a lunch table just talking to total strangers and they'll make you think of the most amazing things."

Larry walked into the room and stood first in line at the counter, watching as the Jell-O was placed on the dessert shelf. Madeleine stood up, still holding my hand, and gestured to Seymour.

"Let's get some lunch," she said to him, nodding towards Larry.

Once in line, she turned around towards Seymour. "So, how are we going to get Jerry an FM transmitter now? There's no way they're going to let us out of their sight now."

Seymour looked around the room. "I suppose we could make one out of scrap electronics parts. I don't know how we'd get a soldering iron in here, but we might be able to just twist the wires together."

Madeleine shook her head. "I don't think Jerry would want to trust his brain to something twisted together."

"Well, you can't just go in the web and have one delivered. I tried that with the parts for my paint bomb. They wouldn't take delivery for things ordered by patients."

"A paint bomb?" Madeleine asked, doubtfully.

"Yeah, it's great. You put a drop cloth on the floor, and tape newspapers to the windows, just like when you paint a room normally. But then you put the paint bomb in the middle of the room, set the timer, and walk out the door. A minute later, boom, the whole room is painted. No sweat, no waiting." Seymour seemed very happy when he was explaining his inventions.

"And you ordered the parts for one and had them sent here?" Madeleine asked.

"Five gallons of black paint, a pound of black powder, a wind-up timer, a flashlight, duct tape, and a box of matches. You see, you break the glass on the light bulb in the flashlight, and tape it to a match head, then stick that in the black powder, and tape it all up really tight with the duct tape. You bring wires out from the flashlight and tape them to the timer, so when the timer winds down, the wires touch. The flashlight turns on, the match lights up, and the paint is delivered in a fraction of a second. Never pay for a painter again. And no brushes to wash out later."

"How do you keep from blowing the windows out?" Madeleine asked.

"Hmmm. Gotta think about that. Needs a little work." Seymour pondered this, looking over at the window.

"It's like being in prison," Madeleine said.

"People sneak things into prisons all the time," Seymour said. "Cigarettes, drugs, liquor, files in birthday cakes..."

"Someone on the outside can bring it in!" Madeleine said. "Like Larry's sister! She comes to visit every Sunday."

Madeleine turned to Larry. "What's your sister's name?"

"Julia," he said. "She likes Jell-O too."

"Everybody likes Jell-O," Madeleine said, although I knew she didn't care for it. People should not lie to Larry. It isn't nice.

"Do you think she could bring us something, the next time she visits?" Madeleine said.

"I hope she brings me a video game," Larry said. "I asked her and I asked her, but she says they cost too much money. I have the bunny game and the beach ball game, and I know there's more games, but I only have those two games."

I was looking up Julia Henshaw in the clinic database. It appeared she had moved to an apartment a few blocks away to be closer to her brother. But Doctor Wilson had limited her visits to once a week, after it appeared that Larry was not responding to his medication. That didn't seem very nice. I changed it so she could visit any time she liked. But I added her address to my to-do list.

Larry's personal effects were listed in his file. I found the video games. A quick search found several similar games by the same company. I placed an order and had them sent to Julia Henshaw's address. I had them gift wrap them, and add a card from me.

There were several FM transmitters that looked like they would work fine. I selected the smallest one, and the most powerful one, and had them both shipped to Julia Henshaw. I added rechargeable batteries.

Madeleine was still talking to Larry. "Do you think she could bring something for Jerry too?"

I put my hand on her shoulder, and turned towards Larry. "Julia will probably bring something for you on Sunday, and maybe something for me too. Something for my hat. Would you make sure those things don't get lost when she brings them here?"

"I never lose stuff," Larry said. "I used to lose stuff all the time, but now I have a tiny little room where nothing ever gets lost. I can see the whole room if I jump on the bed. But Mary Elizabeth won't let me jump on the bed anymore."

We got our lunch and walked back to the table. "You know the smoke detectors in the rooms?" I asked Madeleine. "They are really cameras. The things that look like cameras are really just fakes."

"Clever," Seymour said.

Madeleine did not sound pleased. "There's going to be one less smoke detector when I get back to my room," she said. "Nobody's going to be watching me getting dressed in the morning. Perverts."

"That's what the memorandum said," I offered. "Why they're shutting down the clinic. Reports of impropriety by members of the staff."

"They're shutting down the clinic?" Madeleine sounded upset. That was bad.

"It hasn't been decided yet. There's going to be a meeting," I said, reading Doctor Wilson's email.

"What's going to happen to us? To you, and your backpack and your hat?" She was definitely upset.

"I don't know," I said. "It doesn't say."

"They can't take away your hat! And what about the program? The medications, the therapy, some people are getting better! It's working for lots of people. They can't just stop!"

"It doesn't seem to be working for me," Seymour said. "Nothing seems to have changed."

"That's probably because you're on the placebo program," I said, reading his chart.

"There's a placebo program?" Madeleine sounded angry.

"Not for Larry or me. But you and Seymour get allergy pills. Oscar gets caffeine pills," I explained.

"So, I'm not getting any medication?" she asked.

"Just something to make you sleepy. That's why you have to take it at night. Larry is getting three times the dosage, because they are sure it should be working for him, but he's not showing any progress."

Larry brought his head close to mine, and pulled the others closer. "Don't tell anyone," he said.

"Don't tell them what?" I asked.

"I don't take my pills," he said.

"Why ever not?" Madeleine said. "Don't you want to get better?"

"You mean smart like you?" Larry asked. Madeleine said nothing. "I see all you smart people," Larry continued. "The smart people are never happy. I'm happy."

"So, you don't take your pills," Madeline said. "What do you do with them?"

"I put them in my crayon box," Larry said. "When I color a lot, the crayons get shorter. So, there's lots of room at the bottom of the box."

"It sounds like something is working," Seymour said. "That's pretty smart."

"We won't tell anyone," Madeleine said. "But can Seymour and I have the pills in your crayon box? And Oscar?"

"Do you have any red crayons?" Larry said. "I'll trade you for red crayons. I used mine all up."

"You can have all my crayons," Madeleine said. "And all of Seymour's, and all of Oscar's."

"It's a deal," Larry said.

"Those dirty sons of bitches," Madeleine said.

I looked at Larry. "I only have half a brain," I said. "But I'm never happy either."

"Maybe it's those pills," Larry said. "But you don't talk funny anymore. They're doing something to you."

He ate his Jell-O, letting each spoonful wiggle in front of his face for a while before each bite. He did seem happy.

"I ordered a couple FM transmitters," I said to the group. "I had them sent to Julia. She should get them before Sunday."

"We need to make a plan," Madeleine said. "What to do if the clinic shuts down. How to get access to the medication. How to stick together as a group. But especially how to make sure Jerry can keep his backpack and his hat."

"They are very expensive," I said. "They cost more money than I have in the bank."

"Maybe we can get some other group to take over the program," Madeleine said.

"Or," Seymour said, "We could see what we can do to prevent the clinic from shutting down in the first place."

Mary Elizabeth walked up to the table. Her voice sounded impatient. "Finish up your lunch, Jerry. You're going to be late for your therapy sessions."

I picked up the last part of my sandwich and stood up. Mary Elizabeth spun around and walked quickly towards the door, and I followed, but only after turning to look back at my friends at the table. Madeleine lifted her arm to wave, but then froze. I waited, and she finished the wave, but was surprised to find Seymour had stood up already.

"Those sons of bitches," she said, and I followed Mary Elizabeth out the door.

Chapter Nine

I sat in front of the computer screen and watched the images go by. I was supposed to hit the 1 key when a happy picture showed up, and the 0 key when a sad one showed up. But I had found out I could link directly to the wireless keyboard with the chip in my head, and so I sat in the chair with my hands in my lap, and sent 1's or 0's at random to make the pictures change. None of them seemed happy or sad to me, but they would not change unless I entered one of those two keys.

Since that task occupied very little of my capacity, I explored on the network while the pictures flashed by. I looked at all the addresses the toy store had in their database. I categorized them by zip code, and noticed that not all the zip codes seemed to match the area codes of the phone numbers given. Many of them seemed to go to post office boxes run by various companies around the country. Some of them were nearby.

I bought several post office boxes and had video games sent to them. Then I sent FM transmitters to them. I had no real purpose, and I was incapable of being amused, but something made me want to occupy my brain with anything but the pictures on the screen. Don't think about the pictures. Find something else to do.

One of my problems was that I did not have enough money to buy my backpack. I looked at my bank accounts, and the trust that was set up to invest the insurance money. I searched around in the computers at the investment company to find out how they made money for my trust. I sorted their accounts by performance, to see what the differences were between high performing accounts and lower performing accounts. Mine was one of the lower performing accounts.

The highest performing accounts were those of three employees of the investment company. My backpack ran analysis after analysis, comparing sales dates of the outstanding accounts against all the others. Don't look at the pictures. Think about something else.

The outstanding accounts seemed to make trades just before large trades in other accounts were made. Then they made trades just after the large trades were made. The trick to making money seemed to be knowledge of when large trades were going to be made in other accounts. I could not tell if I was allowed to do the same thing. To find out, I collected all of the information about the trades, and the correlation analysis I had run on them, and sent them in an email to the local district attorney. I used the email account of the top earning of the three employees. I would check back later to see if the district attorney said it was all right to play the same game.

If the clinic closed, we would need another source of the medication that sped up the brain repairs. In all of the clinic's trials, the medicine seemed to be doing very well, and it was clearly helping me. I looked up the supplier, and looked through their customer records to see if any other clinics had any supplies, but only our clinic was receiving it. It was a custom formulation. The formula was encrypted, and meant nothing to me even after I decrypted it, but I sent it to three other competing suppliers and asked for quotes and delivery estimates. I gave each one a different post office box to deliver the medication to. I used Doctor Wilson's name and digital signature.

I played around with the video from the camera over my head. I looked at myself facing the computer. I recorded several minutes of the video. Then I played the recording back into the video stream, and stood up and stretched my legs and arms, and did some exercises while the pictures flashed by, and the recording of me sat quietly with its hands in its lap.

When Mary Elizabeth came back to get me, I was once again sitting quietly in front of the computer. My hands were now back on the keyboard, and I was hitting the 1 and o keys with my fingers. The last picture stayed on the screen as I stood up to leave. My feet did not move when I expected them to. My head stayed facing the computer screen. The picture seemed to hold me in front of it. I felt a tear falling down my cheek, but I could not determine why it was there.

Mary Elizabeth pulled on my arm, and I turned with an awkward jerk and followed her out the door. Another tear fell down my cheek, and I erased the memory of the picture.

We walked down to the lab, where Doctor Wilson and Doctor Davis were waiting to recharge my hat. The gurney with the straps was ready, and Mary Elizabeth pulled down a fresh sheet of paper over it from a roll at the top.

"Why do I have only one hat?" I asked Doctor Wilson, when he turned around towards me.

"What's that?" he said.

"Why do I only have one hat?" I asked.

"You only need one," he said.

"But if I had two hats, then I could wear one while you recharged the other," I explained.

"Yes, I suppose, but there is really no point. We wouldn't have any more for you to do, anyway. There are only so many tests we can run before your body gives out and you need to rest." He walked over to the computer monitor, and Mary Elizabeth pulled me over to the gurney. I started to lie down, but could not make my legs cooperate. Doctor Davis pushed them down after Mary Elizabeth had strapped my chest to the gurney, and together they pulled the straps tight across my thighs and ankles.

"Ok now, looks like we're ready," Doctor Davis said, and reached for my hat. My arms jerked against the straps, and I felt pain on my tongue and tasted blood. Then it was dark, and the screaming man was sobbing as I slipped away into black oblivion.

When my hat slipped onto my head nine hours and forty-one seconds later, my chest ached, and I spoke out involuntarily.

"Sylvia!"

"What did you say?" Mary Elizabeth asked, turning towards me, after releasing the straps at my ankles.

"Someone's name, I think," I said. My eyes were crusty with dried tears, and I wiped my face on my sleeve.

"Might have been a glitch when the processor came up," Doctor Davis said. "Could be worse, could have been Tourette's." He smiled and winked, and walked out the door.

I was hungry again.

He walked right back in a moment later, followed by a man in a dark brown suit and a black tie. He didn't have a name tag, so I didn't know if I knew him.

"Some people are here," Doctor Davis said to Mary Elizabeth. "They want to talk to everyone. Even the patients. They're from the police."

Doctor Davis did not sound happy about this.

"Do we get breakfast first?" I asked.

"No," the man in the dark suit said. I was pretty sure I didn't know him.

We walked down the hallway towards the conference rooms. There were lots of people there, and several who did not have name tags. The dark suit stopped me when we were in front of the second conference room, and he put his hand on my shoulder and guided me into the room. He didn't seem to want to talk much.

Madeleine and Larry looked up at me when I entered. Seymour didn't recognize me, and Oscar had his head down on the table and was pretending to snore out of boredom. Three other patients were also in the room, but I could not see their name tags.

"You weren't at dinner last night," Madeleine said. "I was worried about you."

"They were charging my hat," I said. "Doctor Wilson says there's no point in having two hats. I can't do more than six hours of tests anyway."

"Doctor Wilson is a jerk. He thinks you're a lab rat. Probably thinks we're all just lab rats. Sons of bitches."

"I'm very hungry," I said.

"We had Jell-O last night," Larry offered.

Madeleine looked up at the rest of the people in the room. "Does anyone know why we're here? Anyone know what's going on?"

"Some people from the police are here," I said. "They even want to talk to the patients".

"If this is about that stupid sex rumor I'm going to be really pissed," Madeleine said. "That could wait until after breakfast."

Seymour looked up at her. "Hi, I'm Seymour —".

"Barnswallow," Oscar finished. "We know. You're famous. Everybody knows you. Especially the people you don't know."

Seymour hesitated, then continued. "They took all the computer technicians down to the station. Arrested them, I think. They sent someone to get some guy who always comes in late. They really got excited when they learned there was a tech who was late. I think someone has been stealing computer equipment."

Madeleine turned from Seymour to look at the door, then back at Seymour. "Did they say anything about damaging cameras?"

Seymour hesitated again. "I heard someone talking about that yesterday," he said. "And smoke detectors."

The door opened, and two men entered. One was dark suit. The other was thinner, and shorter, and was not wearing his suit jacket, but had it slung over his shoulder.

Thin man pulled a chair towards him, and turned it around and sat on the seat back, one foot on the seat. Dark suit remained standing.

"Sorry to keep you all waiting," thin man said lightly. "We just wanted to get everyone in the right rooms for a chat."

"I knew that," Oscar said, raising his head off the table. Dark suit turned towards him, but didn't say anything.

"Are we arrested?" Larry asked.

"Some of us are," Oscar said, and Madeleine hit him on the shoulder.

"We're just here for a friendly chat," thin man said. "we'd like to know if any of you noticed anything suspicious or unusual, especially relating to computer use, or people keeping strange hours, working longer than usual, or anything odd."

"You say that every time," Oscar said, rubbing his shoulder. "As if you don't remember where you are."

"Have we met before?" the thin man asked, turning towards Oscar. Dark suit had never turned away.

"Bet your ass," Oscar said. "And you're never any smarter the next time."

Thin man leaned forward to study Oscar's name tag. "Oscar Wolloughby," he said, writing the name down in a pad he took from his pocket. "What previous encounters have you had with the Cyber Crimes Division?"

"See what I mean," Oscar said, turning to Seymour. "He's got no clue. Some detective, eh?"

"Please, just answer the questions," thin man said. He seemed to be trying to ne nice, as much as dark suit was trying to be menacing.

"Or what? You'll arrest me? We go through all that, and then I end up right back here, and you still don't know squat. You want answers? Ask the big guy here," Oscar said, pointing to Larry. "He's the only one in the whole place with an ounce of sense."

Dark suit took a step towards Oscar. "Answer the questions," he said angrily. Oscar ignored him.

Thin man waved his hands. "No problem, no problem." He studied Oscar's name in his notebook, trying to place him. He looked up at Larry.

"So, big guy," he said. "See anything out of the ordinary?"

"You mean you guys?" Larry asked.

Dark suit spun around and made an explosive sound of exasperation. "Don't be an idiot!" he said.

Larry looked concerned. "You don't seem very happy," he said to dark suit.

"Don't get smart with me!" the big man replied, slapping his hand on the table.

Larry stood up, and leaned over the table, his face inches from the other man's face, studying it. "I wish you would make up your mind," he said softly.

Thin man put his hand on dark suit's shoulder and pulled him back from the table. "I think we've gotten off on the wrong foot here," he said.

Larry sat back down, and Madeleine reached over to put her hand on his arm.

Thin man continued. "Someone from this building, possibly in the computer staff, has been hacking into military sites, banks, government offices, and corporate data centers, at all times of the day and night. We're asking you if you have seen any activity around the computers at strange hours, or any other suspicious activity."

He looked around the room. I started to speak, but Madeleine cleared her throat loudly just then, and said loudly "Um, what was your name?"

"I'm lieutenant Rogers," thin man said.

"Um, I think," she said, hesitating, "I mean, someone with half a brain," she said, and paused. I thought maybe she was frozen, but her hand was moving, "would cover up something like that, and not let you people catch on to them. Wouldn't they have a lot to lose? Getting arrested, I mean, they wouldn't be able to see their friends anymore, or if they were sick, they wouldn't be able to get special medical treatment. So don't you think no one would know about them, so they wouldn't get caught?"

Thin man shook his head. "These guys are brazen. They don't seem to be making any attempt to cover their tracks. It's like they either want to get caught, or don't care if they're caught."

Seymour looked over at Oscar. "Or maybe they're so good they just make it look like they were hacking in from here, when they're really in Poland or the Czech Republic."

Dark suit swung over to Seymour. "What do you know about the Czechs?"

"Don't you guys ever use the Internet? Everybody knows about those guys. Hacking into everything, setting up botnets, spamming the whole world. They probably look for places with lots of computers and lots of bandwidth, and then route their hacks through there."

Larry looked up at Rogers. "Can we have breakfast now?"

Rogers looked at dark suit, and then at each of the people around the table.

"Thank you for your assistance. Please keep an eye out for suspicious behavior," he said.

"You'd think with all the computers the government has, they'd be able to catch hackers by computer, and not have to send out the police to ask questions before breakfast," Oscar said.

"Those who live by the sword shall die," Madeleine said, her hand frozen in mid-gesture.

"Probably from somebody shooting them with a gun," Larry said, nodding seriously.

Rogers and dark suit left the room. The others got up to follow.

"By the sword," Madeleine said, looking startled to see everyone standing up.

We walked down to breakfast in silence, Madeleine holding my hand. In line waiting for eggs and bacon, she asked me, loudly enough for the others to hear, "Do you think the cops will be listening to all our conversations now, using the smoke detectors?"

I shook my head. "They don't have microphones, just video."

"Still, I would think that whoever was hacking into computers all over the place would stop now, since they know they're being watched," Madeleine said, squeezing my hand.

Seymour nodded. "If it was one of those guys with chips in their heads, maybe we gave them a hand back there. I saw where you were going with that stuff about guys with half a brain."

"Enough said," Madeleine said. "Let's just talk about breakfast for a while, until someone invents a good way to have a private conversation."

Oscar piled bacon on his plate. "When someone does, they'll probably call it a Barnswallow," he said.

Chapter Ten

We were watching television after breakfast when the funny little man showed up again. He was standing in front of the television, but I could still see right through him. Or around him, or something. He appeared solid and opaque, but he never blocked my view.

"Good, the relay is working," he said. "A few more, and we'll have continuous communications."

"How much time do we have?" I asked.

"Another half hour of this crap," Oscar said, "before they actually start doing the news."

"Twenty-two minutes," said the funny little man, ignoring Oscar.

"I'm going to go to my room for a little bit," I told the group.

"Hope everything comes out Ok," Oscar said. Madeleine hit him in the shoulder.

I walked down the hallway. "You don't have to vocalize, you know," the funny little man said. He seemed to float down the hallway just ahead of me. "You can just text me."

"That would be much more convenient," I texted. "But the police may be watching the data stream."

The little man disappeared. Little blue balls with words on them started appearing all around me. My backpack began to assemble them into text.

"There are ways to communicate that will look like random noise to anyone eavesdropping. At least anyone eavesdropping that doesn't have the software installed in your main processor. Why is someone listening to your data stream?"

I moved the words on the balls around to form my answer. "I was exploring on the network, and it attracted attention. From the police. They arrest people who do that."

"Use this method, and send your data through the relay. They can't follow it that way. Not for another couple centuries at least, judging from their pace of progress." Something about the little blue balls still seemed familiar, as if I was looking at the funny little man's face. He seemed to pick up on that.

"Once this method has been fully integrated into your main processor, it will look just like the old communication method," he said. "Your main processor is much slower than your backpack, but it is much more capable."

"We tried to make the police think the traffic was from the Czech Republic," I said. "From some botnet organization there."

"Foolish," the funny little man said. "That network was taken down weeks ago. The police will know that. But we can put one back in place there, and cause some trouble, to keep them from bothering you."

"The clinic is going to shut down," I said. "I'm going to lose my backpack, and I won't be able to think anymore."

"That would not be good," the funny little man said. "I'm counting on your continued cooperation. We will need to make sure that you remain connected to your backpack, at least until we can get the repairs completed on the main processor."

"If I had enough money, I could buy myself a backpack," I said.

"Then there is no problem," the little man said. "You have access to all the banks in the world."

"I can't steal the money. That would be wrong," I said.

"I admit it might cause complications. But I see you have deeper issues with this solution. No problem, there are others. Since you can easily decrypt communications, it should be an easy task to make money in the stock market based on what you hear."

"Is that legal?" I asked.

"You want to limit yourself to legal options? Those generally take longer. But there are several ways to make money from intelligence no one else has. You can collect rewards for information leading to the apprehension of criminals. You can sell products no one else knows how to make. You can simply sell knowledge. Collecting the money without attracting attention to yourself can be tricky. Setting up a front company is probably a good idea."

I thought about this. "I may need the money pretty quickly."

"Then you might consider taking the money from someone who isn't supposed to have it. Those people seldom complain to the police. And taking money from criminals might not be illegal, depending on the jurisdiction."

"I think I want to talk to someone else about that, first," I said. "I'm not sure about it."

"As you wish. We have thirteen minutes left. I have a lot of data to download, and it takes longer when we're whispering. Are you lying down?"

I got onto my bed, and put my head on the pillow, holding onto my hat tightly.

"Ready," I said.

The world did not go dark this time. I could still see the room, and hear voices down the hall. But my backpack was very busy processing the data, and I could not think very clearly at all. I decided to sleep until it was all over.

In a little less than thirteen minutes, it was done, and I found I was sweating. I went into my small bathroom and splashed water over my face, and began to feel better. I changed my shirt, and went back out into the hallway.

The new data was about *things*. How to make things. How to make things that make things. Which things had to be made before other things. Which things could be made with things that were already available. Interspersed with the information were notes from the funny little man. Notes like "This can be sold to make money," and "you need to make this whether or not it makes money."

It was a long list. There were only one or two things I knew how to start doing. I was going to need help.

Seymour and Madeleine were not watching television. I wandered around looking for them. I found them playing eight-ball in the employee's break room. I watched them play for a while. My backpack started drawing lines in my vision between the pool cue and the balls and the pockets. I could tell when the shots would miss, because the lines did not end up in a pocket or at another ball.

As Madeleine was racking up the balls for another game, I turned to Seymour. "Could I get your help with an invention?" I asked.

He looked surprised. "You want my help?" he asked.

"I have some ideas," I said. "It isn't an invention yet, which is why I need a real inventor. But if I tell you what I'm thinking about, do you think you could invent something from it? Maybe start a company to actually build your invention? I have some money I could give you to start up the company. I'd do it myself, but I don't know how."

"I already have a company," Seymour said. "Barnswallow Unlimited. We're all set in that department. We can outsource all the manufacturing to China, so we don't need plant and equipment. What do you have in mind?"

He pulled his notebook out of his ever-present backpack and opened it to a blank page. I began to draw. "It's a way of making really tiny things that all join up together all by themselves to make something bigger. You start with a DNA strand — that part I already know how to do, I have the codes and I know of several companies that can make them to order, and put them into bacteria or yeast. But then I need a way to grow those, and give them these elements in forms that don't kill them, and I need a compatible substrate, and something like this..."

I continued drawing. Madeleine and Seymour looked over my shoulder, asking questions occasionally, sometimes jumping in with answers to my questions, or anticipating my words.

"So, when we get this thing built, what do we do with the little bits?" Seymour asked.

"They can do lots of things," I said. "But the first thing has to be the optical rectenna array. This guy builds the quantum dot diode, and this one attaches two metal rods, a quarter of a wavelength long, for several different wavelengths, from infrared to ultraviolet. Then this guy arranges them on the striped conductors, so the rectified current comes out the bus, here..."

"It's a solar collector," Madeleine said. "Made from tiny antennas and tiny diodes. People have been talking about building those for at least a decade. Do you really think they will just self-assemble like that?"

"I think it's worth a try," I said. "If it works, we can call it a Barnswallow."

We spent the rest of the morning setting up the business. We decided to use yeast, since it was easy to find breweries that could grow them in large quantities. I ordered the DNA over the net, and we found a company that could build the substrate panels, and the nutrient baths. We sent out for quotes from biotech supply companies for the nutrient media. By lunchtime, we could think of nothing more we could do until the modified yeasts were delivered.

I waited until lunch to discuss the faster method of making money.

"Suppose," I said to Madeleine, as the three of us ate sandwiches and chili, "someone could go to a bank, and quietly transfer money from the account of some criminals, and put it into another account. Would that be a bad thing? Or would it be a good thing, since the criminal would not have as much money to do bad things with?"

Madeleine frowned, and her foot pressed down on mine under the table. "That sounds like it would be dangerous. The police could track down where the person was, like they did this morning. And the criminals probably could too. And they would not be as nice and polite as the police were."

I nodded. "So, it might be dangerous. That is something we can work on. But is it wrong?"

"Isn't it bad enough that it's dangerous?" Madeleine asked.

Seymour took the other side of the argument. "I think some things are dangerous, like falling off a cliff, but people with parachutes can do it. And the payoff might be worth it. All these guys with chips in their heads are going to be hard up if the clinic closes down."

Madeleine looked up. "Seymour, you do realize that there's only one, don't you? Only Jerry here has a chip in his head."

Seymour considered the information, but did not acknowledge it. "Isn't one enough? My point is that if he can't come up with the money, he's not much better off than the guy jumping off the cliff. And that backpack isn't cheap. If it were me, I would be less concerned with whether it was wrong or right, and more concerned with whether it was possible."

I held up my hand. "I don't want to do it if it is wrong. And I don't want to do it if it puts my friends in danger. And I think I can do it without putting myself in danger, but I might be willing to take longer odds with my own safety than with yours."

Madeleine sat for a long while, holding my hand. I think she was looking at me. "I don't think it is morally or ethically wrong to steal money from people who are doing bad things with it. If they stole it from someone, it would be wrong not to give it back to the original victims. But if it was drug money or extortion money or political graft or something like that, then yes, I would probably consider it a fine for bad behavior. But how are you going to make sure it isn't dangerous?"

"Hiding the tracks on the net is something I can now do, I think perfectly. The problem is the money itself. People are very good at tracking flows of money. But there may be a solution."

"Money laundering," Seymour said. "Well, maybe if you stretch the definition. The idea is to give the money to some charity, and then steal it from them later. At the same time, we make it so the criminals are not in a position to reclaim the money. They would be in jail, or they would be too intimidated by the people they *thought* had stolen the money. Like a rival criminal organization."

Madeleine smiled. "You're Ok with stealing from a charity?"

"Not stealing," he said. "Loaning them money. And we can leave them a little something extra to make up for the disappointment when it comes time to collect. Although it might be fun to leave a whole lot of money from Columbian cocaine lords in the coffers of the Republican National Committee and see what they do with it."

"Some would say that was evil," Madeleine said, looking over at me.

"Well, then we just do the charity loan part, with a real charity. And half the money goes to some guy high up in the rival gang, so they blame him and don't go looking for the real thief."

Madeleine seemed to get more interested in the idea. "So where do you find all these crooks?"

"In the FBI database," I said.

"Jerry! After all that noise this morning?" She kicked me under the table.

"I learned how to do it safely. No traces."

"You realize we'd be co-conspirators. We're equally at risk, just by talking about it," Madeleine said.

"I won't do it if you both aren't on board," I said. "If you have other get rich quick schemes, let me know. We're going to need money for the Barnswallow soon after I buy a new backpack."

"And how do you plan to get the money to Seymour's company without drawing attention to the fact that it's stolen money?" Madeleine asked.

"Pre-orders," Seymour said. "People pay up front for the product, then we build it and ship it. But the people paying up front are just us, with lots of little orders over the Internet."

She shook her head. "Let's think about all of this long and hard before we jump into anything. Let's see what we can do that is safe and legal first."

Later that afternoon, when I was sorting computer images of kittens and puppies into categories of happy and sad, Mary Elizabeth came in and stopped the test. Lieutenant Rogers was standing behind her.

"Jerry, this gentleman would like to see you for a few minutes. He has some questions to ask you." Rogers looked around the cubicle as if memorizing every detail, and then selected the only other chair in the room and sat down as Mary Elizabeth closed the door on her way out.

He looked at me for a while without saying anything, and then cleared his throat.

"It seems that all of the network traffic involved in illegal activities here in the lab was somehow filtered through the address associated with the computer you carry around in your backpack," he said.

I said nothing.

"Who has had access to your backpack computer in the last five days?" he asked.

I sat still in my chair. Then I began reciting an alphabetical listing of all of the people in the lab.

"Wait a minute," he said, after I had listed 33 names without pausing for thought. "All of those people had access to your computer?"

I explained. "Over half of my brain is missing. The backpack is essential for my consciousness. There are long periods when it is disconnected. During that time, I cannot think."

"You can't think without the backpack?" he asked.

"That is correct."

"So, what, I'm talking to a computer right now?" he asked.

"That is correct."

"Get out of town!" he said.

"I am not permitted to do that," I said.

He looked down at his notebook. "So, all these people can use the computer in your backpack any time they want?"

I continued reciting names from where I had left off.

"Ok, ok, enough of that. Who could have accessed the computer, or I mean you, um, at three fifty-three in the afternoon the day before yesterday?"

I began reciting the list again from the beginning.

"All right, all right, enough. Let me think for a minute." He flipped through his notebook as if it contained some clue about how to talk to a stubborn computer.

"Has anyone added any programming to you in the last five days?"

"Yes," I said.

"Who?"

"The funny little man," I said.

He wrote that down in his notebook. "Does this guy have a name?"

"No," I said.

"Does he work in the clinic?" Rogers was getting excited.

"No," I said.

"So, someone who doesn't work here has been adding programming to you?"

"Yes," I said.

"Was he a visitor? Did he come in with someone?"

"No," I said.

"He did it remotely?"

"Yes," I said.

"Some guy can access you any time he wants and upload programs?"

"No," I said.

"But he did at least once," Rogers said, tapping his pen on the notebook.

"My software has been upgraded," I said.

"You're saying it won't happen again?"

"That is correct," I said.

He tapped the notebook again. "Where did he get all those passwords?"

"I do not have access to the information you request," I said.

"Could you tell if he tried to use you again?"

"Yes," I said.

"If he tries it again, could you contact me?"

"No," I said.

"Why not?"

"I do not have your contact information," I said.

"Oh." He thought for a moment. "Do you use phones? Or should I give you my email address?"

"You should give me your email address," I said.

He recited his email address slowly, as if he were speaking over a long-distance telephone connection to someone for whom English was not their first language.

"If he contacts you again, you'll send me an email, right?"

"I can do that," I said.

He flipped through the notebook again.

"Well," he said, "we still have some loose ends. Why would someone use you instead of some other computer?"

"I do not have access to the information you request," I said.

"There are all these computers all over the place here. They could have used any of them. But they used you. Who do you know that's not here in the clinic?"

"Amy," I said.

"Amy who?" Rogers wrote the name in his notebook.

"I do not have access to the information you request," I said.

"Anyone else?"

"Sergeant Leo Martinez," I said.

"Who's he?"

"He is a policeman."

"What's your relation to him?"

"I was standing. He was prone," I said.

"Prone? You mean lying down? What was he doing?"

"He was holding his testicles," I said.

Rogers stopped writing in the notebook. He thought for a moment. He might have been smiling. He chose his words carefully. "What led to that particular situation?"

"Sergeant Leo Martinez is not adept at dealing with people who have brain malfunctions."

"I bet. I'll keep that in mind."

He flipped through his notes again. "How about these other people. William McDonald?"

Something seemed to jump inside me at the mention of the name. But there was no recognition, and no recollection of anything to do with anyone having that name.

"I do not have access to the information you request," I said.

"Henry Monaghan?"

Nothing. No inner jump, no recollection.

"I do not have access to the information you request," I said.

"You don't know your own father?" Rogers asked.

"That is correct," I said.

"Sylvia Monaghan?" he asked.

The muscles in my stomach knotted, and I could not move. Something was trying to take control of my muscles. I could taste blood in my mouth, and feel the pain of my teeth biting into my tongue. My breathing had stopped. My vision began to close in until all I could see was Rogers' face, surrounded by grey checkerboard patterns. An alarm started to beep in my backpack, and then the world went dark.

The straps of the gurney were pressing into my chest and thighs when my hat was placed on my head. All of my muscles were sore, and my tongue hurt.

Doctor Davis was sitting at a computer looking at formatted dumps of my backpack. Doctor Wilson had just replaced my hat, and Mary Elizabeth was watching two computer technicians setting up test equipment in the small room. She did not approve of crowding, but she seemed to be the only superfluous person present.

"Nothing external," Doctor Davis said. "No network traffic, just voice processing and visual stimuli. But there was a huge spike of sub cortical right before the crash. Lots of traffic to peripheral voluntary motor areas."

One of the technicians had graphs appearing on his screen. "Major cortisol spike. Endorphins, epinephrine, nitrous oxide, big blood pressure crash."

Doctor Wilson looked up. "Any sign of what the trigger might have been? What did that idiot cop do in there?"

I said "Sylvia Monaghan". Nothing happened. No response from the screaming man, no frozen muscles, nothing.

"What was that?" Doctor Wilson asked, looking over at me.

"You asked what the trigger was. That was it. He said those words." I tried saying the words to myself, trying to see any reaction. There was nothing.

"Post traumatic stress response," Doctor Davis said, entering something on the keyboard. "Connected to a recall fragment pathway. Crap, is this going to happen all the time now, as the systems integrate?"

"The machine learning program should route around it," Doctor Wilson said. "The isolation protocols kick in, and the predictive coder should see them coming. When the harmful areas haven't been accessed in a long enough time, the bad patterns should be lost, and that area can be integrated without problems."

"You mean if I don't think about it, I'll forget," I said.

"Well, something like that, but not really," Doctor Wilson said. He preferred it when his lab rats did not speak.

"You called it, doc," one of the technicians said, pointing to a graph on the monitor. "The predictive coder is going full tilt. It's painting whole sections down here as off limits."

Doctor Wilson turned towards the technician. "Let it run its course. When it settles down to background levels, run the fight or flight stimulus series and the pre-trauma emotive series, and see if we get any spikes. And whatever series he was running when the cop came in, that will have to be re-run, and it will all need calibration runs for at least an hour before any data collection."

"What if it spikes?" Doctor Davis asked. "It's going to be nine or ten o'clock before the data collection starts."

"Don't call us," Doctor Wilson said to the technician. "If it spikes, just strap him down for a recharge and we'll pick it up in the morning."

"You got it, doc," the technician said, with a mock salute.

When the two doctors had left the room, the second technician looked over at the first one. "Fuck. Like I don't have any plans for the evening. I'll call the nun, you set up the calibration runs. We really should push for getting overtime."

When Mary Elizabeth came back into the room, she unstrapped me from the gurney, and helped me stand up. It hurt to stand up, and hurt more to walk, but I picked up the backpack and slipped my arms into the straps and fastened the Velcro. I followed Mary Elizabeth down the hallway to the testing room.

She left me in the room facing the monitor. There was nothing on the monitor for several minutes, and I spent the time massaging my muscles and probing around in my backpack's memory to try to figure out what the new code was doing. I didn't like the idea of forgetting. I remembered nothing prior to waking up in the clinic, nothing about my accident or anything before it. Since then, as far as I could tell, I remembered everything. I liked remembering everything.

The monitor started displaying pictures. I remembered these pictures. Now I knew this was the calibration series. I did not know what that meant.

Eventually, the pictures changed. I remembered this series also. It had faces of angry people, guns, snakes, spiders, and some things that seemed to have nothing to do with the others, like a garbage dumpster, a naked woman, a dead crow, and a hospital.

That series lasted a long time. It was followed by a completely incomprehensible series of peoples' faces (which of course I could not process), buildings, street signs, pictures of cars, children's books, and a zoo.

I was hungry and tired and sore, but the pictures kept flashing on the screen. Finally, Mary Elizabeth came to get me, and she took me to my room. She seemed annoyed at the late hour.

I placed my backpack next to my bed, and held onto my hat as I undressed and slipped under the covers.

Chapter Eleven

I dreamed. I don't remember ever dreaming before. I was asleep, and snippets of action played in my head. My backpack does not sleep. It records everything. It can analyze what I see in the dreams as the dreams are happening. It tells me when things are not possible, when scenes don't follow other scenes in the proper sequence. It counts how many times a sequence is repeated. It has no idea what to do with the information, it merely records it, and catalogs it, and makes notes about things that are wrong.

Most of the dreams are wrong in some way.

Lieutenant Rogers is in the dream. He is bothering Madeleine. He is on the ground in a fetal position. He has become Sergeant Leo Martinez. My tongue is swollen and I cannot speak. Madeleine is asking me questions. Madeleine has a gun. She is at the zoo, which has become a school building. Madeleine has become a spider.

The dreams are not images like a video. They are concepts, waiting for some part of my brain to fill in, to color into images. That part of my brain is not cooperating. It is not accessible. My backpack is not letting it connect.

Something is very sad. My backpack doesn't feel sad. I don't think I feel sad. But there is weeping, there is loss, there is hopelessness, there is failure. I can't do anything about it. I have the sense of trying, fighting, and being continually frustrated. But I keep trying. I won't give up.

When I woke up, I still hurt all over. I stayed in bed, massaging my muscles gently. My tongue was swollen, and I was very thirsty. I had missed dinner again, but my thirst was much stronger than my hunger. I got up to get a drink from my bathroom sink.

Something in the mirror startled me. I stood there, looking at my reflection. All the parts of my face were still just parts. I could tell my backpack to show me the world upside down, and I could tell that the sink and the lights and the door were all upside down, but I could not tell if my face was right side up or not.

But something had startled me. Something either recognized my reflection as a threat, or as something it had not expected to recognize. I watched my reflection as it filled the glass, and raised it to the mouth in the mirror. I drank. I refilled the glass and drank again. The feeling was gone. I could not find it to analyze it further. The backpack could replay all of the inputs, but the feeling did not accompany the playback.

Mary Elizabeth came into the room, but could not see me in the bathroom. She left without saying a word. But I knew how and when to go to breakfast, I no longer needed her for that. I looked at the shower in my bathroom I had never used. I was always clean after having my hat recharged, and I had never thought about how that happened. But it occurred to me that my sore muscles could benefit from a hot shower.

I turned on the water, and waited for the hot water. I adjusted the temperature, and stepped in. There was no soap or shampoo, but the hot water did seem to make my muscles feel a bit better. I kept my hat above the spray, and held onto it with one hand.

There were no large towels, so I had to dry off with the small hand towels by the sink. I got dressed, and walked out to the breakfast room. There was no line, as everyone had already served themselves, but there was still plenty of food to put on my plate. Madeleine got up from her seat as soon as she saw me, and came over to stand in line while I helped myself to breakfast.

"You missed dinner again," she said.

"Lieutenant Rogers was asking me questions, and one of them caused my backpack to crash," I said.

"He what?"

"Does the name Sylvia Monaghan mean anything to you?" I asked.

She shook her head.

"That was the question that made my brain disconnect from my backpack," I said. "I have a father named Henry, but that did not bother my brain. Sylvia Monaghan has the same last name. I don't know if we are related. But my brain reacted strongly to the name. Now it does not. My backpack has learned how to ignore the screaming man when that name is mentioned."

"Who is the screaming man?" Madeleine asked. "The astronaut? Did you use to be an astronaut? Was that a memory?"

"There is a part of my brain that gets control at the moment when my hat is removed, just before my brain stops working. It usually screams. I think it struggles physically. That's why they strap me down. It can't think. But I think it remembers, and it feels things. Emotions. My backpack blocks him, so I can't remember, and I can't feel things. Or something else blocks him, I'm not sure."

"Like repressed memories. Like what happened in your accident," Madeleine said.

"Or something that happened before that. Something very sad. I don't think the accident was sad. I think it just happened."

We walked back to the table. Seymour and Oscar were arguing with Larry.

"What's the problem?" Madeleine asked.

"He's rationing the pills," Seymour said. "I said we should divide them up, give each of us equal amounts. He wants to hand them out two per day."

"The doctor said only two, you can hurt yourself if you have more than two. One in the morning, and one before you go to sleep. It used to be just one, just before breakfast, but then they said maybe I was too fat, and I needed more, but Doctor Davis said it was really dangerous, and Doctor Wilson said do it anyway."

"You don't trust Seymour and Oscar to take only one pill a day?" I asked.

"They want to take two. They aren't fat. They want to be smart too much, they are going to take all the pills too fast." Larry was adamant.

"What do you say, boys?" Madeleine asked. "Sounds to me like he has you pegged. If you OD on these things, the staff is going to know we're not on the placebo. And then they'll make Larry take the pills under supervision, or by injection. Then we'll all be screwed. I'm with the big guy on this one."

"That means you too," Oscar said.

"I want the cure more than anyone in the world," Madeleine said. "That's why I trust Larry more than I trust myself. If it starts working, *when* it starts working, I might be tempted to rush things."

I ate my breakfast while they discussed the matter. I went over my curiosity list and added a few things, and re-prioritized things. I added some items to my to-do list. The top item on my curiosity list became Sylvia Monaghan. I started a search, but there were lots of Sylvia Monaghans on the Internet, and lots of S. Monaghans. I did not have a middle name or middle initial. I looked for co-occurrences with Henry or Jerry, but found nothing. There was nothing about Jerry Monaghan that looked like it was about me either. I didn't know what Jerry was short for, but none of the names I tried looked like they might be me.

But Lieutenant Rogers had found them. I went out to several local police stations, and found the Cyber Crime Division, and downloaded everything I could find. Personnel records, database search queries, evidence records, network caches. I would look through it all later, once I had everything. My backpack was sorting, categorizing, and analyzing as the data downloaded, but my backpack did not know what to look for. Neither did I.

Seymour was working on his smart phone, reading his email. He interrupted my trance with a question.

"How can they get the iron nanoparticles spaced evenly on the striped substrate?" he asked.

I dug into the data the funny little man had left me. "There's a short bit or RNA that binds to the stripe at one end, and the iron at the other. It is polarized, so running a current through the buffer solution will orient the molecules with the electric field gradient. The ones that have the right spacing will bind, the ones that don't will be washed away. After 8 to 10 cycles, the yields should be good for six nines."

"How about you answer their email, then," Seymour said. "I'm not sure I got all of that."

I found Seymour's email account, and found the message from the manufacturer. I sent the full account of the process. It was too big to send in one email, so I broke it up into three parts.

Lieutenant Rogers had a cell phone that had a GPS receiver. I started a background task to track his movements. Perhaps locations that he visited would relate to Sylvia Monaghan. I looked through his caseload to see if any of the other cases were related to mine. There was a new case, involving a new computer fraud ring operating out of the Czech Republic. I could see the hand of the funny little man at play there.

"My sister called me last night," Larry said. "She says she has a present for me from one of my friends. But I don't have any friends. I just have her."

"You have us, Larry," Madeleine said. "You're my friend. Can't I be your friend?"

"Me too," Seymour said. "I don't have any friends either, nobody ever sticks around for more than ten seconds."

"Seymour's your friend too. He just can't remember who you are," she said.

"Seymour got me a present?" Larry said, looking from Seymour to Oscar and back to Madeleine and me.

"I'll bet it was him," Madeleine said. "But he'll forget who it is for. But we'll see on Sunday, won't we?"

Oscar wasn't having any of this. "Only friends I ever get are people that want something," he said.

Madeleine smiled. "A friend in need is a friend," she said, her hand halfway to her face.

"I guess no one can argue with that tautology," said Oscar.

"Indeed," Madeleine agreed.

After breakfast we went into the employee break room, so Madeleine and Seymour could have a rematch on their game of eight ball. Larry's favorite part was the break. After that, he lost interest, and left to watch television.

Oscar and I watched the game, but my attention was on Rogers' cell phone data, watching his movements. He had started moving from a residential neighborhood towards the police station. I assumed he had spent the night at home, or at the home of a romantic partner. The police personnel files had listed him as single, but I would not expect them to record if he was dating, or whom.

The files did have his license plate number, and the make and model of the car, and I amused myself by trying to find all of the networked cameras along his route, and download pictures of him driving to work.

Clandestine surveillance by occasional traffic camera worked in high traffic areas, and autoteller cameras worked when he was near banks, but there were many long periods where all I had were the GPS updates.

I could try to correlate his movements with the case files I had downloaded from the police database. He was working on two cases, and his division had eight cases in progress. But if he wasn't working on my case, I might never find out anything more about Sylvia Monaghan, or why she was so important or frightening to the screaming man. The Czech ruse might be working too well. They may have given up on me as a suspect.

I looked through the case files for something I could use to get Rogers' attention. Neither of the two cases he was assigned to looked suitable. But one of the eight dealt with large sums of money moving between banks out of the country.

Unlike the Cyber Crimes Division, I had no problems getting into the records of banks in other countries. I didn't need warrants for banks in this country. I didn't need passwords. All I needed was the bank account number listed in the case file.

Of course, that account led to others. I began building a graph of the connections, adding what I could find about the companies that claimed the accounts, and who owned those companies. I was not an accountant, but my backpack kept adding up numbers and noting discrepancies and coincidences.

Seymour won the game, and Oscar stepped up to rack the balls. Madeleine came over to stand next to me.

"I had a dream last night," I said.

"A nice one I hope," Madeleine said.

"I don't know. It is the first one I remember ever having," I said.

"Really? This is like a breakthrough or something? New signs of progress?"

"I'm not sure. When the screaming man got control, I think some connections got made that allowed him to dream. Or allowed me to see his dreams. Or allowed me to dream. I can't tell." In my backpack, the bank account data was starting to make patterns, but I had no idea what they meant.

"But isn't the whole point to get more and more of your brain connected? All the parts that got separated in the accident, and all the new parts the pills are growing?" She was talking quietly, almost whispering, like she wanted this conversation to be only between the two of us.

"The funny little man says the damage repair is going too slowly. He tries to speed it up by making more connections. But the backpack has software that isolates and shuts off areas that cause it trouble. It's like they are working at cross purposes," I said.

"You have all those people in your head," Madeleine said. "All those parts of your brain seem to have their own personalities, and their own agendas. I hope when they're all connected up, you don't end up a schizophrenic."

"Maybe I'm already a schizophrenic," I said. "How would I tell? Everyone seems real to me. But I think being a schizophrenic might be better than being in a persistent vegetative state."

"Well," said Madeleine, "I don't think I'm a hallucination."

The bank account data started to make some sense. The transactions seemed to be happening in one time zone, regardless of which time zone the banks were in. That narrowed the scope to the western United States. I started tracing where the data packets originated, using the methods I had learned from the way Rogers had found me. The data was being routed through anonymizing servers in the Netherlands, but when I had enough data, a pattern started to emerge, and I could correlate the traffic by the times and sizes of the packets.

The information was leading me away from the original bank account. The person I was following seemed to have several schemes running at the same time. Perhaps he was a money launderer for hire, and not the actual person of interest. But I kept building the profile and pinning him down. He might lead to any number of criminals I could use to bait Rogers. Or he might be bait enough in himself.

Rogers himself was standing in front of an ATM at the moment. He was waiting behind a young blond woman who was making a deposit. The camera caught him running his fingers through his hair and straightening his shirt.

When the woman finished and Rogers got up to the ATM, I had a name for the money launderer. I made a decision, and did a little bit of extra investigation. I knew how to get Rogers' attention, and get him thinking about me, without giving him any proof it was me. I accessed the receipt printer in the ATM.

THE GIRL'S NAME IS SUSAN PETERS. HER PHONE NUMBER IS YOUR NEW BANK BALANCE. BUT THE PERSON YOU SHOULD BE WATCHING IS WARREN JENNINGS. HE JUST MOVED 28 MILLION INTO BANCO DE LA REPÚBLICA IN COLOMBIA. THAT'S THE MONEY YOUR FRIEND DAVIS HAS BEEN FOLLOWING FROM CAYMANBANKINGSERVICES.COM.

Just to make sure he actually read the receipt, I added enough blank lines to make it a foot long.

"I'm pretty sure you're not a hallucination," I said to Madeleine.

Rogers was looking around somewhat frantically. He left the ATM and I no longer had visual of him, but he was apparently running in a direction other than towards his car. Perhaps he was chasing down Susan Peters, suspecting her of having left the note in the ATM somehow.

It was my turn to play. Seymour had won again. I racked the balls as I had seen Oscar do. I don't recall ever playing eight ball before, but I knew the rules. Seymour did the break.

I watched the balls roll across the table. My backpack superimposed lines on the table, predicting the paths of the balls. When I picked up the cue stick, I was surprised by the weight of the heavy end. It felt clumsy and strange in my hands. I positioned the cue in front of the ball the way I had seen the others do. As I moved the point of the cue, the lines on the table moved. The line from the cue ball curved right and left as I moved the cue to either side of the ball. I waited until the lines showed a ball going into a pocket, and pulled back the cue. The lines moved wildly. I adjusted my aim again, so that the lines found a pocket.

When I pushed the cue forward to meet the ball, the lines moved again, and the ball went wildly in a direction I had not anticipated. My muscles had not learned how to move the cue in the proper way.

Rogers was back in front of the ATM now. I watched as he checked his balance. I could not tell if he was disappointed that it no longer showed nine digits. I could still not read faces, and that is a severe handicap.

Seymour had made his shot. I stepped up to the table again. This time I only moved the cue back an inch, and tapped the ball in the direction I wanted it to go. The line on the table ended just in front of the pocket, and the ball stopped right at the end of the line.

"Ooooh, almost," said Madeleine, putting her hand on my shoulder. Seymour stepped up to take his next shot.

Rogers was in his car, judging by the speed he was traveling. I plotted his probable course, and watched traffic cameras. He was heading to the police station. The first traffic camera that caught him showed a flashing light on the dashboard of his car. It seemed I had caught his attention.

Seymour won the game easily, and the rest of the day was fairly uneventful. Rogers was very busy, making lots of phone calls and sending lots of emails. Doctor Wilson had me scheduled for hours of time in front of the computer monitor watching images flash by and hitting 0 or 1. I kept sending random sequences while I continued tracking the activities of Warren Jennings, trying to build up a list of his clients and profiles for each of them.

I was in bed that night when the funny little man appeared again.

"I almost have the next relay in place," he said. I could watch him floating near the ceiling as I was aware of him uploading large amounts of data from my backpack. He was not pleased with what he was finding.

"There are whole areas not being exercised," he said. "The repairs are going fine where there is traffic, but if we don't get data going to these parts, they will never integrate."

"I think my backpack is preventing them from being accessed," I said.

"That won't do," he said. Seconds went by as the upload continued. "Yes, here it is. This won't do at all. Protecting the crutch at the expense of the patient. Look at this. The major portion of the motivation circuits are all being routed around. How can anyone expect rational behavior if the processor can't care about the outcomes? It's detecting emotional responses as errors instead of as inputs into the values matrix. This is going to need work. It's all wrong."

"My backpack processor crashed yesterday," I said.

"I can see that. It's fighting the repair process. The code was written to be in control, and when the main processor starts to take control, it sees it as damage. This is going to take time to fix. I can make a few tweaks now, and help speed up the repairs a bit in the short run, but building a whole package will have to wait for the next orbit."

"Are you a hallucination?" I asked.

"Of course I am," he replied. "I'm not here, you know. I'm three hundred miles over your head, and closing."

"Am I a schizophrenic?"

"No. That's an entirely different kind of damage. Not something I could work with. Not useful at all. Oh, good, I see you've started the manufacturing process. You should probably get started on the ribbon in parallel with the panels. No sense wasting time."

"But they both use the iron nanoparticles, and those aren't ready yet," I said.

"Get two companies working on them in parallel. Then you have a second source if one of them slips the schedule. How's your other little project going, getting the money for a backup processor?"

I hesitated. "Madeleine thinks it is too dangerous," I said.

"You do have physical security issues," the funny little man agreed. I could tell he had revised the isolation protocols because my stomach knotted a little bit when he said that. But my processor did not crash, and the screaming man was quiet.

Chapter Twelve

The next morning at breakfast, Larry was excited. It was Sunday.

Sarah Henshaw always brought the Sunday funny papers in for Larry. He never seemed to get the jokes, but he loved looking at the pictures.

"She's going to bring my present from Seymour today," Larry said.

Seymour looked up. "That's my name too," he said. "Seymour Barnswallow. I invent things."

"Speaking of which," I said. "I have another project I'd like to get going."

"Getting money to buy a backpack computer?" Madeleine asked, a little suspiciously.

"No, this is another use for the iron nanoparticles. It uses them as catalysts for making carbon nanotubes. But this is a process for making them arbitrarily long, and forming billions of them into a wide ribbon," I explained.

"A ribbon of nanotubes?" Madeleine asked. "Like for a space elevator?"

"I don't know what it would be used for," I said. "I just know how to make it. But we'll need to get a different company working on it, so both projects can proceed in parallel. That way, if one of them hits a snag, the other one can supply some technology or product to the other."

"I hope it's a rabbit," Larry said.

"Hope what's a rabbit?" Seymour asked.

"My present," said Larry.

"It's not a rabbit," I told him. "But you're going to like it."

"I could take care of a rabbit," Larry said. "I could feed him, and give him a bath, and pet him. And I wouldn't squeeze him too hard. They don't like it when you squeeze them too hard."

I sent an email to Seymour with the data for making the ribbon.

"Of course you wouldn't squeeze him," Madeleine said.

Just before ten o'clock the four of us were waiting in the lobby for Sarah Henshaw. Larry saw her walking up the path to the big glass doors and started hopping up and down. She was carrying a grocery bag in one hand and the comics section of the newspaper in the other.

"Hey, Larry," she said as she came in the door. She wrapped her arms around him in a big hug, the bag and the newspaper rattling and banging together behind the big man's back.

We walked back to Larry's room. He kept trying to peek inside the bag, but she made a game out of hiding the contents, and then slightly opening the bag again, as if by accident.

The first thing out of the bag was Larry's video game. He squealed when he saw it, and worked furiously at unwrapping it, while simultaneously looking around for his game player. Sarah helped him get the wrapper off, and set up the game, and then Larry was oblivious to anyone else in the room, his attention riveted on the tiny screen, delighted by the sounds each button press created.

Sarah brought out the second game, and set it down on the bed behind Larry. Then she pulled out my FM transmitter boxes and several packages of batteries.

Madeleine opened the smaller box while I worked on the larger one. As soon as I put the battery in mine and flipped the switch, I was aware of the signal from it. The chip in my head read out the received signal strength level as I played with the tuning until I got the optimum value.

The transmitter I held was the more powerful one, but it still fit nicely in my front pocket, and the chip in my head was happy with the power level. I turned it off, and Madeleine handed be the smaller one. I turned it on, and spent some time tuning it. It was able to power the chip if I kept it within about a foot of my head. Any farther than that and the only signal the chip could read was that from my hat. It was like the chip locked on to one or the other, but would not accept power from both.

Madeleine took off her necklace and put it around my neck. "We can hook it onto this," she said, "and it will always be within range."

I turned the transmitter off, and tucked it down my shirt collar on its new chain.

"So, are you going to try it without the hat?" Seymour asked.

My stomach tightened, and my mouth watered. I considered the idea, but the screaming man was having none of it. However, I was still able to function.

"I think I'll wait until I have no choice," I said.

"You probably only want to have one transmitter on," said Seymour. "That way, if the battery starts to run down, you can turn the other one on while you get the new battery in."

"Good idea," Sarah said. She was watching Larry enjoy his new game. "I really want to thank you guys. Look at him. He's so happy."

"He's the happiest person he knows," I said.

Sarah looked at me. "He told you, didn't he." she stated.

I nodded. Madeleine said "Yes."

"Don't tell anyone. Please don't tell anyone. He'll change his mind eventually, but don't let them kick him out of the program. He needs the stability, and we really can't afford to keep him anywhere else." Sarah was holding Madeleine's hand.

"We won't tell. Everyone loves Larry," Madeleine said.

Sarah stayed through lunch, and then it was time for me to do more tests. I sent random numbers to the calibration test, but when the actual test began, something new happened. I stared at the picture of a lop-eared white rabbit and thought about Larry and his desire for a pet. I reached for the keyboard and pressed the 1 key with my finger. There was something about the rabbit, something that made it obviously a 1 and not a 0. Something that made me want to acknowledge it, and not just send a random number.

Some of the pictures were mildly disturbing, and they got an immediate zero. Others evoked no immediate reaction, and I waited for something to happen before sending a random one or zero to get the next picture.

I had planned to follow Lieutenant Rogers during this time, but the task at hand was suddenly interesting to me. I decided to try doing both. Rogers was at the bank again, this time inside. Through the security cameras I could see him with two other policemen talking to men in suits with bank nametags. The picture was not good enough to read the nametags, even when I zoomed in.

I felt the muscles in my back tighten as an image of a gun appeared on the test monitor, at the same time that I was looking at armed policemen who were trying to track me down. The fact that I wanted them tracking me down did not seem to matter to the muscles along my spine. This was another new experience. I don't think I liked it. There was something comforting about not caring. *You can't get hurt if you don't care.* The concept formed without words, but the meaning was clear.

The funny little man seemed to think it was very important to be able to care about things. My backpack seemed to disagree. The screaming man seemed to care about things, but it didn't seem to be getting him very far. I could not tell if the wordless concept was coming from my backpack or the screaming man, or from something outside of the room. But I wanted to ask it a question. If I didn't care if I got hurt, would you care?

At the bank, I could see men taking apart the autoteller from the inside. They would find nothing. Perhaps Rogers could think of nothing else to do. I clicked some ones and zeros as I went back to the computers at the police station. There was an address there that had not been there in my first visit. Perhaps someone had left a laptop computer plugged into the network?

I started scanning through the files at that address. As I did so, network traffic suddenly grew, and then died out as machine after machine disconnected from the network, and routers shut down.

The new address was a trap, a honey-pot. As soon as it was accessed, alarms went off in the station, and routers shut down immediately. I could see the packets from the investigation computers trying to track down where the intruder had come from.

Back at the bank, Rogers' cell phone was ringing. The policemen all left the bank in a hurry. I could see Rogers' GPS trail heading for the station.

A naked woman appeared on the test monitor. She got a one. On a scale of zero to one, it was the highest score she could rate.

An idea came to me just then. I liked this idea. I routed my packets through the router in Warren Jennings' office. I then started scouring all the files on the honey-pot trap computer at the police station. The original entry would not lead them anywhere, but this new one left a trail a good boy scout could follow all day.

It would lead right to Warren Jennings. And the police would have grounds for issuing a warrant to search his computers. I disconnected and went back to concentrating on the image test. Maybe there was another naked lady in the sequence.

After a little over an hour of pressing ones and zeros, I received an email. A company in China had responded to our request with a quote. I wired the money right away to get them started. I checked my account balance. I could do a few more of those, but after that I would need more money. And I still did not have the money for a new backpack computer.

As a test, I decided to steal some money. I would not actually keep it myself, so there could be not money trail leading back to me. I would steal it from one of Warren Jennings' clients, and move it to another of his clients. After sending half of it to the Save The Rainforest Foundation.

I did it from the honey-pot computer. Rogers would love that.

Rogers had not yet connected any of this new mess to me. If he didn't make the connection, he would not investigate me, and I would not find out any more about Sylvia Monaghan. I said the name to myself a few times, trying to get a reaction from the screaming man, but he seemed to be immune now. Perhaps coming from me it was not a threat.

The image tests were finally over, and Mary Elizabeth came in to tell me it was time for dinner.

Dinner was nice, although Larry spent the entire non-Jell-O part of dinner with his video game, making his own beeps and buzzes along with the game. But the rest of the group seemed to enjoy seeing him so happy.

After dinner, Mary Elizabeth led me into the lab to recharge my hat. I reached into my pocket and turned on the larger of the two transmitters. The other one was still on the chain around my neck. I was tense, but it was different from the rigid muscle-lock that happened when they usually strapped me in. This tenseness came with anticipation. I wanted to see if it would work.

Doctor Wilson and Doctor Davis were both in the lab, looking over my test results. "Looks like you had a breakthrough today, Jerry," Doctor Davis said. "The new code seems to be working great. You're actually getting decent scores."

I said nothing. I knew that it was the funny man removing the new code that actually made the difference. Removing the new code, and the old code.

They helped me onto the gurney. "Look," Doctor Davis beamed. "No resistance! This is real progress!"

They pulled the straps tight, and Doctor Davis reached up and removed my hat. Nothing happened. I was still there. I could still think. The transmitter was working.

I wondered how long the battery would last. I could not reach up to turn on the second transmitter if the first one should fail. Bad planning.

I played dead. Apparently, this was a new experience for the others in the lab, and they seemed very pleased. I wondered what normally happened when the hat was removed.

They all left the room and turned out the light. I was alone, and cold. There were no covers, and the room was air conditioned to keep the computers cool. I could not move to get comfortable. I could flex my muscles, and I tried rubbing my arms and legs against the gurney to generate friction.

I went out on the network to see if I could get the machines in the lab to work harder, and generate more heat. But then I found the central air conditioning controls, and I turned up the heat in the room, and shut off most of the machines so they wouldn't overheat and generate alarms. In a few minutes, I was more comfortable. I increased the heat more, to make up for the lack of covers.

The next time they strapped me in, I would raise my arms and legs just a little, so I could later relax them and the straps would not be so tight. It was going to be a long night.

A little after midnight, I fell asleep.

Chapter Thirteen

I woke several times during the night. Each time I checked the power levels my chip was getting, and each time I went back to sleep not knowing whether I would wake on my own, or would wake to the feel of Mary Elizabeth fitting my hat on my head.

But I was still awake and had power when she came into the room in the morning. I reset the temperature, and continued playing dead. Doctor Davis came into the room, and I could hear him taking my hat out of the charger. Mary Elizabeth placed it on my head, and I opened my eyes.

"These straps are too tight," I said. They both ignored me, but Mary Elizabeth started undoing the straps. When my arms were free, I reached into my pocket and turned off my transmitter.

I sat up. My muscles were not stiff and sore, but I stretched slowly and carefully, imitating my previous performances.

At breakfast, Madeleine was excited to hear about my night. "It worked! Seymour, you're a genius!" She hugged Seymour, who seemed to have guessed that she already knew him and did not introduce himself.

I went online and ordered more transmitters and lots more batteries. I wanted my friends to have them, just in case.

"Next time, I'm bringing a blanket," I said. "I wish I could do something about the straps being so tight."

Seymour thought about this. "I think we could rig that. A little S shaped piece of metal or strong plastic. We could weave the straps in it to take up slack. Then, after everyone was gone, you could pull the gadget out, and the straps would be loose. Probably just need to do it on the strap that holds your hands down. Then you could loosen the others with your free hands."

Madeleine looked at Seymour and then over at me. "Or one of us could just sneak in after lights out and undo them for you."

"Well, yes, I guess so," Seymour said, sounding a little disappointed.

I checked in on Warren Jennings. His network address did not seem to work anymore. As if the police had raided his office and taken his equipment. I checked the police station. Their routers were back on, and I compared the addresses with those I had seen the previous two times, and identified the new honey-pot traps. Checking the activity logs, I saw that Jennings had indeed been raided the previous night. Nevertheless, he was out on bail already.

They would notice the bank transfers when they handed the records over to forensic accounting. I wondered if Rogers would be surprised to learn the transfer had been done at his computer. He had started changing his password every night, and using his thumbprint to log in. Of course, that made no difference to me.

"Maybe you were an astronaut before your accident," Madeleine said again. "The carbon nanotube ribbon — that is what someone would need to build a space elevator. Or, you could have been a physicist working for NASA, or a chemist. That's how you would know how to make one."

"Or an inventor," Seymour said.

"But if I was, wouldn't I know what the thing could be used for? I don't know what a space elevator is."

"It's a ribbon of super strong material that is anchored near the equator somewhere on earth, and anchored to a big rock somewhere past geosynchronous orbit at the other end. A tractor grabs the ribbon and climbs all the way up into outer space. Building it is a bitch, but once you have it, getting into space is really cheap."

"But the funny little man is already up in space," I said.

Larry looked up from his game. "Maybe he wants to come down. Like Jack and the Beanstalk. Maybe he's stuck up there with a goose."

"Or maybe," I said, "he's the giant."

We finished our breakfast talking about Sarah's visit, and Larry's new game. He hadn't opened the second game yet. The first one would probably last him months.

There was a spasm in my foot. I don't recall anything like that happening before. I looked down at my foot.

"Is something wrong?" Madeline asked.

"My foot just moved," I said. "All by itself. Just a little jump."

"That happens sometimes," she said.

"Not to me."

"Oh." She hesitated. "You're not taking too many of the pills, are you?"

"No, just one a day," I said. I moved my foot. I wiggled it up and down and side to side. It felt normal.

In my head, I could hear a song. This was also new. I listened for a while.

"Do you hear music?" I asked.

Seymour shook his head, and Madeleine said "No".

"I hear music," I said. "In my head."

"Maybe your chip is picking up a local station," Seymour said. "Sometimes that happens to people with fillings in their teeth."

"I don't think it's a radio," I said. "It doesn't sound like a song on the radio. It repeats parts, and parts aren't really there."

"Like an earworm," Madeleine said. "A song that's stuck in your head."

"There does seem to be a song stuck in my head," I said. "It was not stuck there before. I don't remember ever hearing the song before."

"If you're hearing a song that you never heard before, it must be coming from the outside," Madeleine said. "Is your transmitter on?"

I checked the one around my neck, and the one in my pocket. Both were off.

"It started when my foot twitched," I said. "I think I am now accessing a part of my brain I could not reach before."

"That's good, right?" Seymour asked. "That's what you're here for, right?"

"I think so," I said. "But it isn't much use, is it? Having noise stuck in your head that you can't turn off?"

Madeleine laughed. "Maybe it just means you're human," she said. "You're becoming more like the rest of us."

That afternoon Mary Elizabeth let up on us enough to let Larry go to the zoo on the bus, but only if she accompanied him. She was not up to leading the whole group, however, and said so. She felt she could trust Larry if he was alone.

It wouldn't have mattered for me, since my afternoon was scheduled for hours of more tests. The doctors were excited to see progress, and they wanted more data for the paper they were going to write. The tests were not particularly interesting, but they kept me busy enough that I could not do much of anything else.

After the tests and dinner, I was exhausted, and I went to bed early. Lying in bed, I had time to think about Lieutenant Rogers. He had still not connected the activity to me, and so he was not investigating Sylvia Monaghan. The only reason to get him to investigate me was to find out more about Sylvia. Perhaps it was time to make him think about her more directly.

I opened an email account with the name Sylvia Jane Monaghan. I had no idea what her middle name really was, but Sylvia Monaghan was already in use. Then I used it to send an email to Warren Jennings. She said she was expecting a large sum of money from a prominent former government minister of Nigeria, and wanted to avoid paying taxes on it. Was he still taking new customers?

Nothing good enough to get a warrant, no real evidence, but Rogers would have to come talk to me about it. Either I did it, or I was being framed by someone who knew intimate details of my life or my conversations with Rogers. I could point to the cameras in every room in the clinic, and point out that any of the computer technicians could have seen the video of our discussion. He would not know there was no audio without checking. He'd probably check, but at least I had plausible deniability. And Rogers thought that I was an idiot, or an idiotic computer program, and so far, he had no reason to expect that I was capable of devious behavior.

Hopefully, he would use the network to contact someone who knew about Sylvia. If he continued relying on personal interviews and hand-written notes, I would get nowhere.

In my dreams, there were no faces.

In the morning, after breakfast, I knew Rogers was coming. He had done a web search for the name Sylvia Monaghan shortly after getting to the station. I could watch his cell phone's GPS location move along the roads from the station to the clinic. But even so, something tightened in me when Mary Elizabeth came to get me.

Rogers wasted no time. Mary Elizabeth has barely closed the conference room door behind her when he looked at me and asked "What the hell is going on?"

"I do not have access to the information you request," I said.

"I think you do. Someone handed us Warren Jennings on a platter. But they also made sure that Norte del Valle thought my precinct had something to do with a lot of their cash ending up in the accounts of Santander de Quilichao. My people are looking over their shoulders everywhere they go today. Jumpy cops are not good cops. They're dangerous cops. This is no game."

I sat quietly and waited for him to ask a question.

"What do you know about Warren Jennings?"

"He is on a platter," I said.

Rogers put his head in his hands. "Who were you talking to about Sylvia Monaghan?"

"You," I said. "And Doctor Wilson, Doctor Davis, and Mary Elizabeth."

The notebook came out, and he wrote down the names.

"What is her middle name?" he asked.

"You did not tell me her middle name," I said.

"That's right I didn't. But of course, you know her real middle name. Someone you talked to, or someone who overheard us would not know her real middle name. If it weren't for that, I'd have you down at the station in a much less comfortable chair. It just so happens that the first Sylvia Monaghan that comes up in a web search has a different middle name. One that showed up in Warren Jennings inbox last night."

Again, I waited for him to ask a question.

"Who might have heard that name when you were talking to those other people?"

"Anyone with access to the camera feeds from the smoke detectors," I said, pleased that I was able to get that into the conversation.

Rogers looked up and the ceiling, and found the smoke detector. "They're watching us right now?" he asked.

"The cameras record all patient activity," I said.

"Who can access the recordings?" he asked.

"I do not have access to the information you request," I said.

"Do they keep logs of who accesses them?"

"I do not have access to the information you request."

"If anyone talks to you about Sylvia Monaghan, I want you to contact me right away. If you even hear the name mentioned, contact me. You understand?"

"I understand," I said.

He got up and left the room. I waited for Mary Elizabeth to come and get me. I waited for a long time.

Rogers had given me names to match the accounts of Warren Jennings clients. I went out to the net to do some research on them. There was a lot of information on the groups themselves, but not very much that would help me track their finances on the net. The FBI and DEA networks were much more helpful.

Wire transfers were easy for me to track, but much of the money was actually transferred as bulk cash, carried across borders by such methods as replacing refrigerator insulation with cash and shipping the refrigerator. Other methods, such as buying cars in the U.S. with dollars, and selling them in Bogota for pesos were also used. I should be able to track those transactions to some extent, using shipping manifests, once I had correlated used car companies with cartel bank accounts. That would take some time. I set it up as a background task in my backpack, and continued my network search.

I set up alerts for any mention of certain names by agents of the FBI, DEA, Border Patrol, and local police stations. If I could determine where any of the known cartel subjects were at any time, I could try to determine cell phone numbers, and perhaps get lucky and track them by GPS as I had with Rogers. I was scanning files on CIA computers when I found a payment to a Sylvia Monaghan. No middle name mentioned. Enough money to buy a nice car, but only the one payment. Unfortunately, I had uncovered 638 Sylvia Monaghans in my searching, and the odds were against this one being the one I was looking for. But I added the Social Security number to my list of Sylvias.

I could see Rogers was on the road again by the time Mary Elizabeth remembered I was still in the conference room. She came in the room, and then stopped, assessing me.

"The bus is about to leave, if you'd like to go to the coffee house. Your friend Amy has been asking about you," she said.

"You're letting us on the bus again?" I asked.

"Just one at a time. Doctor Wilson thinks you're all bad influences on one another, but he says you don't get into trouble when you're on your own. So, are you coming?"

"Yes," I said. "I'm coming."

Larry was on the bus already. But Madeleine, Seymour, and Oscar were not. Mary Elizabeth followed me up the steps, and the bus started off on the familiar route to the coffee house.

"They said I could see the bunnies again," Larry said. "I won't squeeze them. They don't like that. But they might let me pet them if I'm really gentle."

The bus stopped at the coffee shop and I got out. They waited until I was inside before the bus left to take Larry and Mary Elizabeth to the petting zoo.

"I was getting a little worried about you!" Amy said, as I walked up to the counter.

"Me too," I said. "But I seem to be trustworthy again."

"That's what I missed," she said. "I never know what you're going to say next. Even when it makes no sense, it still sounds so smart. I think you're my favorite customer."

"I think you're my favorite Amy," I said.

I ordered the artichoke heart quiche and a glass of milk.

"No chocolates today, OK?" Amy said. "Remember what happened last time!"

I sat at my usual table. No one else was in the coffee shop. I opened my laptop computer and set it up in front of me, although I didn't need it anymore. But I tried to match my earlier routine. Amy would get worried if she saw me simply sitting at the table staring into space.

I started reading Rogers' latest updates on the Warren Jennings case. He had not had time to file anything about the morning interview, but my name was prominent in the report, and the clinic was ground zero for his part of the investigation. Someone at the clinic was feeding the police information on money laundering by Colombian drug cartels. Or someone wanted the police to think that the information was coming from the clinic. He suspected the first clumsy hacking attempts were actually a ruse to draw attention to the clinic, since the perpetrators obviously had technology that enabled them to remain undetected when they wanted to.

Someone else was reading the report at the same time I was. I followed the packets, expecting to find a computer in the station I could add to my list of non-honey-pot machines I could search through. But this person was outside the station. I traced the packets back to an anonymizing server in Sri Lanka. Someone did not want to be found.

Anonymizing proxy servers prevent police from tracking packets because they exist in jurisdictions where the police can't get warrants. But for someone like me, with the funny little man's toolkit, that was no problem. I traced the data flow through the server, and out to the net to another one. In all, eleven servers were being used, some in Japan, some in Russia, some in Europe. I finally got to a computer outside of Chicago, and knew I had my hacker.

The first thing I did was to prevent any new programs from being run on the target computer, so that I would not trip any honey-pot traps. I went lightly into the files, not using up enough bandwidth to alert the hacker that someone else was using his machine. All I wanted were the files that had been modified in the last few hours. But I set up a script that would upload the entire contents once the machine had been idle for more than an hour.

I also set up a program on the server of his service provider, to forward all of his traffic to me. He would not be able to see that happening, since it was upstream of him. He was using three layers of encryption, and he may have thought that gave him some protection. But anyone who could decrypt one could decrypt the other two. All it really ended up doing was slowing down his access to the network.

I collected a list of all the addresses his machine had sent packets to in the last ten hours. It was a very long list, but I knew what I was looking for. I compared the addresses from his machine with those I had found on Warren Jennings' machines. There were a large number of addresses in common, but I could rule out addresses this list shared with lists I picked at random from other computers I did not suspect of having links to drug cartels. This eliminated large numbers of computers that delivered common services like email and web search. My target list was getting smaller.

"Here's your quiche," Amy said, bringing me a plate and a glass of milk. "I made sure it isn't too hot."

I smiled and thanked her. She stayed for a moment looking at me. It occurred to me that I had never smiled at her before. I could not tell what she was thinking. Faces were still impossible for me to read.

I was going through my list of addresses one-by-one when my target made life easy for me. He was sending the police report to one of the addresses on my list. It would be interesting to see how this hacker-for-hire was paid for his services. I put looking through his bank records near the top of my to-do list. But for now, I followed the report to an address on a mobile phone.

Someone was reading the report on their mobile phone. I got the phone number, and the GPS location. He was on the street in front of the police station. I accessed the security camera at the front of the station. I could see the cars parked across the street, but I could not read license plates, because none of them were facing the camera. But I could see that two of them looked occupied. I saved the video for later, and added that cell phone to the list of phones I was tracking, which now numbered two.

I started collecting a list of traffic cameras, ATM cameras, security cameras, and web cams around the police station. I would be ready when he started driving. His movements would let me know which car he was in, and if I was lucky, I would get a shot of his face and license plate from a traffic camera.

The phone was using a pre-paid card, so the customer record would be unreliable. Indeed, it claimed to be owned by Susie Smith of Orlando Florida. But the phone had been activated from a pay phone in Santa Monica, California, three days ago. But I already knew this guy did not want to be found.

I was still having no luck with Rogers. He was not looking into Sylvia despite my efforts. I was slowly collecting data on all the Sylvia Monaghans I could find, but nothing I was getting led back to me, or to anyone named Henry Monaghan. Rogers knew her middle name, but I could not think of a way to get him to tell me without letting him know I didn't know it already. I was regretting not simply asking him in the first place, but that would not have fit the 'dumb computer' image I was trying to project.

I set up a web site. I put what I had about the hacker-for-hire reading the police report, the cell phone it had been sent to, and the video from the camera at the police station. When I had a plate number or a face, I'd add that too. I set it up so that it asked for a password. Anything entered would work, but the password would be stored where I could get it later.

Next, I created a new email account for s_monaghan_01, and used it to send Rogers an email.

> *Someone other than me has been hacking into your files. I've put the information about how to find him at the web site shown in the subject line of this email. He sent a copy of your police report on Warren Jennings to someone also described on that web site. I suspect that second person is one of Jennings' clients. The password for the web site is my social security number. Sylvia.*

With Sylvia's social security number, I should have no trouble getting more information about her.

Cell phone number two was on the move. As he drove, I quickly located more cameras along his route, and got several short videos of the car, the driver, and the license plate number. The plates were registered to a local used car dealer. I would not be surprised to learn that the car was rented for the day using cash and a false identity.

The car drove directly from the station to the clinic. A short while later, I was getting nice video from the smoke detector cameras in the lobby. I added all of this new data to Sylvia's blog.

I was not the only one watching the video. The hacker-for-hire was copying as much data from the clinic as he had bandwidth to take. He was not being particular. Which meant he was not getting anything of much use to him, since the clinic had enormous stores of medical scans, dumps from computers like my backpack, and results from experiments. However, as that thought had barely crossed my mind, I watched as he downloaded the personnel files of the staff, and the patient records.

The man I was calling cell phone two was chatting with the receptionist. She began handing him brochures from the display by her desk. I watched as she added business cards to the stack of color glossies in his hands. He looked around the room again, in a leisurely way, and I saw him waving goodbye to the receptionist as he walked out.

I added that video, and a log of what the hacker had downloaded, to Sylvia's blog.

Cell phone two gave me an unexpected bonus. He stopped at an ATM and withdrew five hundred dollars in cash. I got a good close-up shot of his face in the ATM camera, but even better, I now had access to a bank account linked to him.

I was starting to trace deposits to the account when the bus arrived, and Mary Elizabeth came in to get me. On the ride back, as Larry regaled me with the events of his day, I was able to find three accounts that had transferred money to cell phone two. I was on a roll. I documented these in Sylvia's blog.

After dinner, I was in the recreation room with the others, the television tuned to one of Larry's favorite nature programs, when the little man appeared again. I got up and quietly left the room.

"Another relay in place," he said. "Now there will only be a few times a day when we're out of touch."

I filled him in on the progress with the solar panels and the nanotube ribbon, and he was impatient as usual. I also explained my search for information about Sylvia, and what that had led to. He seemed less interested in my personal life than in the projects.

What interested him was progress on the repairs to my 'main processor'. The pills were stimulating brain growth, but it was the use patterns that directed where the growth would occur, and he thought I needed to exercise areas of my brain that were slow in coming online. Those areas consisted of parts where the damage had been most severe, and areas that my backpack had been cordoning off. There was little to do about the former other than wait for it to repair itself. The latter areas, however, were ready to be integrated.

"You're learning to care about some things," he said, "and that is excellent. But there are a lot of other things you need to care about. You need to re-learn how to fear. Otherwise, you won't survive. You've been living according to rules instead of emotions. Emotions are essential to functioning. They provide the motivation, the goals, the reasons to take action. You go through the motions, but you have no desire to win, no fear of losing. You need those."

I told him about my curiosity list. I showed it to him. It listed all the things I had heard about in the last four days but did not yet know. It had Sylvia, criminals, bank transactions, and all the other thousands of things I had discovered I did not know.

"Without emotions, you have no way of ordering the list," he said. "If you had real curiosity, you would not need the list. But curiosity is a mild emotion. To get things rolling, we'll need to get you connected to strong emotions. Those will be the ones that have the most intact connections left, and the ones most likely to generate new connections fastest."

I did not mention that I had no idea how to generate those strong emotions. Let alone milder ones. I went back to the recreation room. If he wanted to continue the conversation, I could participate silently. People around me were used to me acting a little distracted.

The television show was about tigers. They were supposed to be fearsome. But I noticed that my companions showed no more fear than I did, as far as I could tell. Of course, I still could not read their faces.

That night, in bed, I dreamed of tigers. I was petting them, and being careful not to squeeze them too hard. They don't like that.

In the morning, the funny little man joined us at breakfast. I had a feeling he was actually busy doing something else, and what I saw was just a metaphor, a way of contacting him if I needed to. I could just turn to him and talk if I wanted. But this morning, I was talking to Madeleine and Seymour.

"I've been practicing moving money around," I said. "But I promised not to actually take any for myself without talking to you first. But I know of an investment account with 28 million dollars in it, and I made a list of 2800 charities that frequently get donations of up to ten thousand dollars. When someone makes a lot of transfers of money that are just under ten thousand, the IRS computers get red flag warnings, since that amount is just under the income tax reporting limits."

"You kill two birds," Madeleine said.

"You get the money, and you burn the bad guys," Seymour agreed.

"With one stone," Madeleine said.

"These guys already have the local police looking into them, and the DEA and the FBI have files on them. Having the IRS in the mix can only help. And they have a rival gang angry with them. Once they have been taken out of business, one way or another, we can steal some of the money back from the charities, and no one will be looking for us."

"And if you are only taking a couple thousand from each charity, it won't hurt their planning process so much," Madeleine said.

"So, do you agree that we should do it?" I asked. "There will be nothing traceable to us until we actually steal it back, and that won't be for a while."

Seymour nodded. Madeleine hesitated, then said "We need to get you a backpack before the clinic closes down. I think this is the fastest way. The other projects won't be ready in time."

I had all of the transactions ready. I set them in motion. A few seconds later, I said "Done."

"Just like that?" Madeleine asked.

"It's just sending some data," I said. "It doesn't take that long."

The funny little man did not seem to be paying attention.

After breakfast, Seymour, Oscar, and Madeleine agreed to help me learn how to get billiard balls to go where I wanted them to. Training my muscles to move the cue properly was much harder than I thought it was going to be. If the funny little man wanted me to desire to win, learning how to play a game that others wanted to win might help.

It was after lunch before Sylvia's web site reported that someone had accessed it. I checked the password. Rogers had either been lazy or clever. He had simply typed the digit 1, and of course the web site let him in.

So, I still didn't have any more leads to Sylvia Monaghan. But at least Rogers was aware that his quarry was also stalking him, and he now knew who to look for. I added the tracking data for cell phone two to the web site. Now Rogers would know where the man spent the night, and where he had been at other times.

Cell phone two stopped sending GPS reports about a half hour later. I loaded the remaining tracking data onto the web page, noticing that the cell phone stopped operating at the airport. It looked like our man either removed the card, or the battery, or both. I would not be surprised if the phone itself had been thrown into a trash can somewhere at the airport.

The afternoon was all tests at the monitor in the testing room. After the calibration sequence, I paid particular attention to the images that were there to evoke emotional responses. I tried to figure out what my reactions were, and what the designers of the test thought the reactions should be in a healthy person. I could identify 'interest' as a reaction, but I didn't know if it qualified as an emotion.

Another reaction I labeled 'amused'. Some of the pictures were just a little more than interesting, usually because there was something incongruous about them. These were probably amusing to healthy brains.

Then there came a series of words in different colors. I was to enter a one if the word was the proper word for the color it was printed in, and a zero if the word wasn't. I was to do this as quickly as possible. The word GREEN showed on the screen, but the word was printed in blue. I entered a zero immediately.

I watched my performance. My backpack could tell me exactly how long I took to enter my answers. It was always the same. I suspected that a healthy brain might be faster or slower if the word and the color matched, or that a healthy brain might answer incorrectly when the colors didn't match. I was always correct, and I was always very quick. I expected Doctors Wilson and Davis would be disappointed. I wondered if the funny little man would care.

I checked on Rogers just before dinner. He was at the airport. I wondered what name our target used to book the flight, and how he paid for it. There were many flights out in that general time frame, and dozens of them were cash transactions. However, if he had suspected someone was following his cell phone around, an airport would be a good place to dump it, before coming back undetected.

At dinner, I watched Larry playing with his Jell-O. The others at the table joked and laughed, and everyone seemed to be having a good time, even Oscar. Like me, Oscar never laughed at jokes. He had heard them all before. But he laughed at people, and he laughed with people.

Was humor an emotion? One of these days, I would be able to laugh. It looked like it would be something I would enjoy. Was it a strong emotion? I couldn't tell.

After dinner I went to my room and carefully folded a blanket from my bed into a small bundle. I carried it into the recreation room and held it while we watched television. Madeleine saw it, and came over to sit next to me. She held my hand while we watched.

When Mary Elizabeth came to tell me that it was time to charge my hat, Madeleine followed us into the lab. Doctor Davis looked at me, holding the blanket.

"What's this?" he asked.

Before I could speak, Madeleine answered him.

"You can't leave someone strapped to a gurney all night without a blanket. It's cold in here, and he'll wake up frozen stiff."

Doctor Davis shrugged and walked over to the keyboard and began typing. Madeleine spread the blanket over me, and helped Mary Elizabeth fasten the straps. She made a fuss over getting them tight, but the straps over my arms were loose enough for me to get my hands free if I desired.

She stayed, holding my hand, as Doctor Davis removed my hat. I played dead. I felt two short squeezes on my hand, and then the three of them left the room and turned out the lights.

Cocooned in my blanket, I was definitely more comfortable than the last time. I had fresh batteries in my transmitter, and spares in my other pocket. I could get my hands free to turn on the transmitter on my necklace if I needed to swap batteries in my pocket transmitter. And the funny little man was floating nearby if I needed conversation. I was feeling pretty good about my situation.

I looked over my lists. My curiosity list was getting quite long. I thought about what the funny little man had said about prioritizing it. I looked for things on the list that correlated with things on my to-do list, and moved them to the top.

The to-do list was also getting pretty long, although I had been much better at getting those things done. The superconducting tape project had yet to be started, but it was high on the list because it was easy, not because it was one of the little man's must-do projects. At least the 180° Celsius version was easy. The 400° version required some technologies that weren't available yet. But they were on the list.

I did some research on companies that had the capabilities we needed, and sent an email to Seymour outlining what needed to be done. It took a lot longer than I expected. It is not always apparent from what you can find on the net which companies could do what you needed. I had to cross-reference scientific papers and their authors with their funding sources, and look into university contracts and NSF grants. But I was able to give Seymour five possibilities to check out.

I was a little after midnight when Madeleine quietly opened the door. She closed it behind her, making as little noise as possible. She did not turn on the light.

"How are you doing there?" she whispered. "Comfortable?"

"Yes, quite comfortable," I said. "A big improvement."

She began unstrapping the restraints at my ankles.

"I think we should leave them in place," I said. "I can move around enough to keep from getting stiff. If the doctors come in and see them undone while I'm still asleep, they might make sure they are tight the next time."

She hesitated, them refastened the strap.

"Did I wake you up?" she asked.

"No, I was working on another project for Seymour. The world is going to have a lot of Barnswallows in a few months."

"That's just like Seymour," she said. "A new introduction every day."

She hesitated, and I wondered if her brain had paused, but then I realized she was waiting for me to laugh. She had made a joke.

"I'm sorry I can't laugh," I said. "But someday soon, I will."

"I'm sure you will," she said.

The door opened and the lights came on. As we were blinking in the sudden brightness, an unfamiliar voice said "Don't nobody make a sound or you're dead meat."

Two men, dressed in black clothing, were standing in the doorway. One of them had a gun aimed at Madeleine's head.

Chapter Fourteen

"Take the chick too," the first man said.

"You," he said, waving the gun at Madeleine. "Turn around and put your hands behind your back. Make a sound and I'll clock you, get it?"

Madeleine looked over at me, and then at the gunman, and turned around. The second man fastened her wrists together with plastic zip ties.

The first man started cinching the straps on the gurney so tight they hurt. I could not move. He pushed Madeleine out the door into the corridor, and then pulled the gurney out after her, with me firmly strapped on to it.

I tried to access the video cameras to send videos of the gunmen to Rogers, but they had been disconnected. Power to the building was off. I could access four cell phones, however, and I used Madeleine's to fire off a message to Rogers.

"Madeleine Hartford and Jerry Monaghan are being kidnapped at gunpoint at the Leo Finklestein Neurology Research Center," I sent. "Two gunmen in black clothing. Native Spanish speakers. Medium height, slightly heavy set. Eagle tattoo on forearm."

I sent the email quickly, expecting the men to search Madeleine at any moment and take her phone.

They rushed the gurney down the hallway to the lobby. Madeleine and the second gunman followed, Madeleine running awkwardly with her hands behind her back. We reached the open door, and the gurney bumped heavily on the threshold, and then we were through the door. A van was outside, the engine running and the back doors open. The men pushed Madeleine into the back, and she landed heavily onto the hard floor. They lifted and pushed the gurney in, and tipped me sideways, the gurney wheels facing the side of the van, my head facing Madeleine's feet.

I was starting to have flashes of coherent thought, followed by a kind of daze, and I realized my backpack and hat were still back in the lab. The chip in my head, powered by the transmitter in my pocket, was barely able to send data that far, and less than half of the packets were getting through. As the doors shut and the van sped off, I lost contact with the backpack altogether.

I could feel the screaming man take over control of my body. The transmitter in my pocket still powered the chip in my head. The chip was still able to connect parts of my brain that had no other connections. The screaming man had many more resources than he had previously, but critical areas such as the speech center were still unavailable to him. He screamed, but no words came out.

The woman was terrified, but tried to calm him. He could not understand what she was saying. This enraged him. He was angry, frightened, and at the same time filled with a tremendous sadness and loss. These were the strong feelings that the backpack had suppressed connecting to, because they overloaded the processor with constant demands for processing power.

The screaming man fought to control himself and understand his situation. He was trained for this. This was not an unfamiliar situation. He took comfort in his training, and began controlling his breathing, and assessing his surroundings.

First priority, get himself free of the gurney. The woman could move around, and use her hands to undo the straps. He tried to tell her what to do, but he could not form words. He started jerking the gurney towards her, nodding his head at the strap across his chest. Frustration and anger threatened to overcome him again, and he worked on controlling his breathing once more. He had to learn how to control his anger. It was going to be a major problem if he could not get it handled.

The woman was not cooperating. She looked at him, but did not understand what she needed to do. He closed his eyes and took deep breaths. He tried working his hands free under the blanket. His fingers could barely lift the fabric. He looked at the woman again. There was something about her face. Besides the obvious fear she seemed to have of him in his current thrashing, angry form, he felt there was something about her face that surprised him. He could not figure out what it was.

If he wanted her help, he would have to reassure her. He had to act rationally, but the anger and frustration were hard to control. It was as if he was under the influence of some drug that prevented his mind from controlling his emotions, and prevented speech.

He took a deep breath, and let it out slowly. He looked straight into the woman's eyes, and winked. She looked surprised, and then smiled. He smiled back. Then he looked down at the straps holding him to the gurney, and back at her face. She finally seemed to understand. She sat up, and pushed herself closer to him, sliding on the floor until her bound hands were close to the strap that bound his wrist to the gurney. She was talking the whole time, but he could not understand a thing she said.

She managed to free his right hand, and that was enough. He quickly freed his other wrist, and then undid the remaining straps and tried to stand up. His numb legs would not cooperate. Then he felt stabbing needles as the circulation slowly returned.

The van stopped, and he could hear both men get out. He tried to stand up, but fell back down immediately as the rear doors opened.

He heard three musical notes and looked over to see the woman hiding her cell phone under the blanket next to the gurney. Her wrists were still bound behind her back, and the two gunmen did not see the phone.

There was a lot of shouting when they saw that he had gotten free of his restraints. He tried to fight back as the two men tackled him, but something was wrong with his muscles. He seemed to be extraordinarily weak, and his body did not work the way he remembered. But his memory also didn't work properly, he could not remember how he got in his current situation.

The men bound his wrists and ankles with plastic zip ties, and pulled him out of the van. They pointed guns at the woman and she came out, standing on the gravel at the side of the road. A dark sedan was parked ahead of the van, and the men carried the screaming man to it, and dumped him on the rear seat. They pushed the woman in on top of him, and got into the car.

The two in the back seat sorted themselves into sitting positions awkwardly. He could see the van pull back onto the road behind him, and make a U-turn, going back the way it had come.

The woman continued to talk. Sounds tumbled from her mouth, but they conveyed no meaning. It did not sound like language, it seemed to be completely random. He shook his head as if to clear away a drugged fog, to no effect. He took a breath, and assessed his surroundings, looking for anything that would provide an edge in a struggle, or some other advantage.

He had something in his pockets. Neither of them had been searched. This seemed amateurish to him. They did not have his training. They were not professionals. He tried to recall what his profession was, but could not. He began to get angry again.

Another deep breath. The drugs would have to wear off soon, as he seemed to have most of his faculties — he could see clearly, and hear, he could plan. But he was amazingly weak, he could not understand people when they spoke, and he could not remember crucial details of his past, either recent or ancient.

The first order of business would be to free his hands and legs. Plastic restraints are easiest to remove by cutting or burning, his training had taught him. An automobile had several methods of producing heat and fire. The easiest was the cigarette lighter, but a hot manifold, a catalytic converter, or friction of a fan belt would do. There were also several ways to produce a sharp cutting edge. Broken glass, the threads on a bolt or sheet metal screw, a windshield wiper blade bent until broken.

None of these solutions presented themselves in the back seat, except for the dome light overhead. He could try breaking it, but he would need to make it look like a side effect of some other action, or he would tip off the gunmen.

He looked at the woman. She carried no purse, and her cell phone was back in the van. He wondered what she might have in her pockets, and whether she could reach them, bound as she was in the confined space of the back seat. He slowly edged closer to her. The gunman in the passenger seat was turned to face them, and he was watching. There was no way to reach towards her to check her pockets. If he started feeling her pockets, she would get the idea and let him know if they contained anything useful. She was alert, and not panicked, which was a great relief to him.

He felt along the seat for anything useful. Any small bit of paper or twig might be used to jam the zip mechanism on the restraints and allow him to pull them apart. There was nothing on the seat, but he slouched down slowly, watching the gunman through the corner of his eye, and tried to reach behind the seat, to where such debris would get trapped. A paper match would do, or a toothpick, or a cocktail straw. He felt only sand and lint. He moved away from the woman, as if shifting to get more comfortable, and tried again. The gunman said something loudly, and waved the gun, but the sounds were unintelligible. The screaming man shrugged his shoulders and sat still.

Amateurs. The gunman waved the gun around in front of him, where it could be grabbed or knocked free. If only he had free hands to do the grabbing or knocking. He might knock the gun free with his head, but there was the second gunman. And the gun might go off and hit someone in the back seat.

The woman was also looking around, plotting an escape. This was good and bad. He would have to be aware of when to capitalize on any initiative she took, since communication was extremely limited. And whatever she was planning might interfere with whatever he eventually came up with. But she was acting like a partner, not like a dead weight, and for that he was extremely grateful.

He could not tell what he had in his front pockets. His back pocket, where a wallet should be, was empty. Why didn't he have a wallet? Car keys could be used as a saw, if he had lots of time. But the lump in his front pocket didn't feel like car keys. He was not aware of hearing any jingling of metal in his pockets when he was pushed around. The woman might have keys.

He could sand the restraints off on the corner of a stucco building, or the concrete edge of a sidewalk, if either of those opportunities presented themselves.

The gunmen wanted them alive, or they would already be dead. They were being taken somewhere to be held. Escape during transit was usually the easiest time. He did not know how long it would take to get to their destination. Professionals would pick a place far enough away to make searching unlikely, but close enough to make the trip a short one, to eliminate the chance of escape or detection. What these amateurs would do was anyone's guess.

He felt around quietly behind the seat. The woman saw what he was doing, and then quickly looked away. Good girl, he thought. If the gunmen ever left them alone in the car, he could kick out a window, free his hands on the broken glass, and hotwire the car. At least he remembered how to hotwire a car. The steering column would lock, but judicious use of forward and reverse would attract attention, preferably police attention, and perhaps cripple or kill a gunman in the process.

The zipper on his pants could be used as a saw. He would have to bend his torso enough to slip his bound wrists under him and then pull his legs through. This might not be as easy as it was in training, he seemed to have gained considerable weight. What had happened to his body?

The woman wore blue jeans as well. He smiled. Without being able to communicate, the idea of pulling her zipper down and rubbing his wrists against it for an hour or two might not meet with her approval.

He turned to ways to signal for help. The cell phone in the van presumably alerted someone. He tried to picture how to work a cell phone, but the symbols did not come to him. The woman could do it, however. He did not know whether she had been successful. But the van was going in the wrong direction. It had probably already been stripped and wiped down, but then again, these guys were amateurs. But the police would not be finding them soon based on what they found in the van.

The car horn could be used as a signal. He could not remember the signal for asking for help. That one should be easy, but it stayed just out of reach. Speech, symbols, communication in general seemed to be impaired. At least he had been able to wink. That was communication.

He was aware of seconds passing. He knew exactly when the van had stopped, and exactly when the car had started, and exactly what time it was at this moment. It was a very strange feeling, as if someone else was telling him the time whenever he thought about it. They had been driving for over three hours now. Definitely amateurs.

The car was driving through open country now, without a lot of street lighting, traffic, or businesses. He could see agricultural buildings occasionally, but it was too dark to tell if they were travelling through cropland.

A half hour later, the car slowed and turned onto a gravel road. Another six minutes, and it pulled to a stop. Two men came out of a single-story building and met the car. They both held guns that he recognized, but could not name. He should be able to name any automatic weapon on the planet, but the words were just not there.

The driver opened the woman's door and pulled her out of the car. The gunman from the passenger seat opened the other door, and the two new men helped pull the screaming man out roughly, the three men getting in each other's way trying to lift him out. They carried him into the building. He scanned the area quickly, assessing it as thoroughly as possible. A large central room, what was probably a kitchen to the left, a hallway to the right. They carried him down the hallway, past a bathroom, a bedroom, and into what may have once been a laundry room. It had a large sink, a drain in the concrete floor, and the walls had been covered in new sheets of plywood. There was a single bed in a corner. The men dropped him roughly onto it. The woman followed, and was pushed onto the bed after him.

The men left the room, and a deadbolt clicked into place as they closed the door.

The screaming man got up quickly, balancing on his bound feet, and nodded his head at the woman to also get up. She had less trouble doing so than he had. He crouched until his hands could grab the bed frame, and he lifted it up until it rested on its side.

The metal edge of the bed frame was not very sharp, but he started rubbing his restraints against it as rapidly as he could. If the edge wouldn't cut, the heat might melt. The woman tried the same thing on the other side of the bed, but she did not seem to grasp the friction heating aspect of the operation, and proceeded more slowly.

As he worked, he scanned the room. Plywood covered every wall to a height of eight feet. He assumed there was gypsum wallboard under it, which would have been easy to kick through. There were no windows, or they had been covered by the plywood. The sink has a black plastic drainpipe that he might be able to use. He could sharpen it on the concrete to make a stabbing weapon. The faucet might work as a bludgeon if he could kick it loose.

The plywood was nailed in place, not screwed. Screws could be undone, and nails could be pried out. The ceiling was usually the weakest point in a room. He could use the bed frame as a ladder, and knock out the gypsum wallboard of the ceiling, getting access to the attic. From there he could crawl over another room and kick his way through the ceiling into that room. Assuming the noise didn't alert guards.

There was a bare bulb in a fixture in the ceiling. That could be broken to get glass shards to cut the restraints, if he could maneuver the bed frame to knock the bulb out. That would be easier if he could talk to the woman and get her to cooperate.

His arms started to ache, but he kept up the pace. The plastic was slowly succumbing to his efforts. If it got thin enough, or hot enough, he could pull it apart by brute force. But he remembered he had little brute force to work with in this new body. What the hell had happened to him?

He slipped the restraints behind the steel leg of the bed frame and pulled hard. One of the plastic bands snapped, at the expense of a sharp pain in his wrist. But his hands were free.

It was easier to rub the plastic binding his legs against the metal frame, but his control of where the plastic met the metal was making up for it. The woman was still working on her own restraints, but not having much success. He was nearly ready to try pulling his leg bands apart when the door opened. He spun around to face the door, ready to attack, bound feet or not.

The man at the door looked around the room, and at the two prisoners, and laughed. He was a new face, not one of the four gunmen, and he had no gun. What he had was a pair of wire cutters. He walked to the woman and cut her restraints off her wrists.

He was talking, and he seemed to be in a good humor, as he approached the screaming man. Preparing to grab the cutters and hold them to his captor's neck as soon as his feet were free, he noticed the guards at the door with their automatic weapons. Better to wait for another opportunity. They might not sleep in shifts, thinking their prison would be sufficient. He waited while the restraints on his feet were cut, and then held out his left hand to have the remaining loop removed.

His captor was making noises. He made the noises again, this time grabbing the screaming man by the chin and looking into his face as he made the noises. The screaming man made random noises back at him, and earned a slap across the face that would have landed hard had it not been expertly blocked. The guards at the door started getting excited.

The woman started making noises. Wire cutters turned towards her. They made noises at each other for several minutes. The screaming man considered his choices. He could grab the man, and use him as a shield as he pushed towards the guards at the door. He would then grab a weapon and hose down everyone in the hallway. He estimated his odd of success and looked for another opening. His new body was not up to the task of moving the fat captor's bulk quickly enough to make it to the door before being gunned down.

The noises got louder, and the fat man called to someone in the hallway. The driver came in, his pistol in his hand. The fat man shouted and gesticulated, and the driver defended himself equally loudly. After a few minutes of this, the fat man waved the guards back into the hallway, and walked out, closing the door behind him. The deadbolt clicked into place.

The screaming man walked back to the bed frame and lifted it away from the mattress. The mattress fell flat onto the floor, and he set the bed frame on end against the wall, the bottom on top of the mattress. He climbed up the bed frame, and started knocking quietly on the ceiling, looking for where the ceiling joists were. He removed one shoe, and used the rubber sole as a pencil to draw lines mapping the joists.

Near the wall, where the bed frame could act as a ladder, was also where the attic would most likely be too small to climb into. The center of the room would be a better place to enter, but the bed frame would have nothing to lean against. He looked around, but the room had nothing to offer.

He set the bed back up as a bed, and went over to the sink. He sat down and kicked at the plastic drainpipe until it came apart. He took one piece over to the woman and handed it to her. He took the other piece and began rubbing it against the concrete.

The woman did not seem to get the concept. He pantomimed rubbing it against the concrete, and then cutting his throat with the sharpened tool. She nodded, and began rubbing hers on the floor next to him. She tried to talk to him, and to pantomime something, waving her fingers in the air, but he could make no sense of it. She kept pointing to his back and making typing motions. He went back to sharpening his weapon.

He stood up and looked at the woman. He pantomimed unzipping his jeans, and pointed to the drain in the middle of the floor. At first, she did not understand, but then nodded her head vigorously, and bent down to her sharpening task with renewed effort. He relieved himself, and then came back and resumed sharpening. She got up, and unzipped her pants, talking while she did so, although by now she knew he could not understand.

While grinding the plastic against the concrete, he continued processing the room. He could break the bulb and get glass to use as a weapon. That would leave the room dark, which might help with the element of surprise, but would probably end up giving even more of an edge to the men carrying automatic weapons.

The light would have electrical wiring in the ceiling to power it. That could be yanked out once he was in the attic, and used as a garrote or a whip, or a tripwire. He could possibly use it as an electric booby-trap if left connected to the mains. The light switch, wherever it was, was covered with plywood and inaccessible. That would make it difficult to construct the trap, especially in the dark. He continued grinding.

The woman was getting tired. Her pace on the grinding began to slow. His arms and back ached, and he cursed this new body that had somehow gotten so out of shape and flabby, but he continued without slacking the pace. It might be a matter of life or death, or it might just be a matter of winning. It was a contest either way, and he was going to win.

He stood up to avoid cramping, and paced the room, swinging his arms left and right to free up the muscles and enhance the circulation. He went to the door and pressed his ear against it, but if there were voices to be heard, he would not be able to understand them anyway. But there were none. The hallway was quiet.

He started rubbing the plastic on the concrete in such a way as to draw a map of the building, such as he had seen. He could cut a hole in the ceiling, and lift the woman into the attic. She could crawl to the adjoining room, and kick through to the room below. She could then come back and unlock the door for him. That way, he would not need to stand the bed on end, but just stand on it to boost her through the ceiling.

How he would communicate all this to her, he did not know. He wondered if she had the strength to lower herself into the room. He doubted she had any martial arts training that would help her fall properly and avoid injury and noise. It was a lot to expect.

His weapon was sharp enough to kill. He admired it for a moment, and then quietly pulled the bed into the middle of the room. Standing on the bed, he pushed the sharp plastic into the ceiling.

Working quickly, he made several stabs along the line of the rafters, white dust falling on his head and shoulders, and on the bed. When he had perforated a neat square, he used the plastic pipe to pry it loose. He grabbed it as it fell, and lowered it onto the bed quietly.

Insulation followed, and he jumped up to grab the ceiling joist, but could not lift his head up to see into the attic. Damn! When did his arms lose their strength? Not a single pull-up was possible.

He motioned to the woman to join him on the bed. She stood next to him, and he grabbed her thighs and lifted her until she could hold onto the joist. He adjusted his grip quickly, and put one hand under her foot, and pulled up. She helped by pulling with her arms, and she looked inside. He gave her some time to get her eyes accustomed to the dark, but then he had to lower her down and rub his burning muscles.

He led her to his map, and tried to pantomime what he needed her to do. She did not approve of the plan. He wondered if he could lift himself up if she were underneath pulling up on his feet. At the very worst, he could climb her like a ladder, his feet on her hips and then on her shoulders. He paced the room again, trying to get his muscles relaxed, and keep the blood flowing. He picked up the square of gypsum and placed it in the sink, and carefully tipped the mattress against the wall to hide the white gypsum dust. He turned the mattress over, and placed the bed back where it had originally been.

If someone came into the room, they might not notice that there was a hole in the ceiling. If he heard someone coming, he could hit the light with his plastic pipe, and plunge the room into darkness. He could stand by the door with his weapon, and plunge it into the first neck that he could see as the door opened, and hope that there was a gun he could quickly grab.

He paced and waited. The woman went over to the bed and stretched out, closing her eyes. It was just before six o'clock in the morning, and he guessed she was tired of the night's activities. Rest could come later for him. If he was to make his escape, his best shot was the moment his captors opened the door, and that would be sometime in the next hour.

He looked around the room, checking again for anything that would give him an edge, stack the deck in his favor. He remembered his pockets, and pulled out the contents. The little device in his hand was familiar. He was holding a transmitter. In the other pocket were extra batteries. The transmitter was on, and transmitting. This could be good or bad, depending on who was listening or tracking the signal.

The transmitter had been in his pocket before the abduction. It may have been how they found him. Or, it may have been there for some other purpose. It was too short range for anyone to track it in a moving vehicle. It may have been sending signals to compatriots outside the building from which he was taken.

It seemed unlikely to be of any help in his current situation. He might use it to send information by turning it on and off in code, but he could not remember how to send code. Whatever drugs they had used were very slow to wear off.

He slid the power switch to the OFF position.

And fell down. He no longer had voluntary control of his muscles. They twitched and jerked in spasms as he flopped around on the floor. His vision and hearing were gone, and the feeling on the right side of his body was gone, leaving him numb on that side. He tried to think, but everything was foggy, and he could not concentrate. Fear gripped him, and he could feel his heart beating fast, and his breathing turning into gasps as he tried to gulp air as quickly as possible.

His vision cleared, and he heard the woman's voice trying to sooth him. He looked at her. She held the transmitter, its red power light once again turned on. She pantomimed — keep this in your pocket, and keep it turned on. He took the device and replaced it where he had found it. His muscles hurt all over, and he rubbed cramps out of his calves and thighs.

He got up and resumed pacing. This new development was too baffling to reason out, and he put it from his mind as he went back to planning escapes. In his current physical condition, attacking the first person in the door would only get him shot. His speed and reflexes were not what they had been.

With day approaching, the ceiling was a long shot. His captors would all be awake, and he would not have cover of darkness for the escape once he got out of the building.

He was still pacing when the first data packets started flashing in his brain. It was like having another person taking control of his body, in fits and starts. The fear came again, followed quickly by fierce, uncontrollable anger. Then the link was complete.

"Christ on a crutch!" I said, startling Madeleine from her perch on the bed. "They brought my backpack!"

Chapter Fifteen

I moved quickly to the door, flattening against the wall, the sharpened plastic ready. "Get into the tub," I said. "Quickly!"

Madeleine hesitated. I whispered urgently, "It's cast iron. It will stop the bullets." Her face showed recognition, and she hurried to the basin and climbed in. I could see her face. All of it, together at the same time. I could marvel at that another time. Footsteps were coming down the hall. Two people. That was good. One would have his hands full with the backpack.

The deadbolt slid back, and the door opened. I grabbed the first man by the shoulder, and pulled him into the room, tripping his feet with mine, and sending him tumbling onto the floor, the backpack still slung on his shoulder. The second man has a look of surprise on his face, my plastic knife embedded in his side up to the hepatic artery, blood pumping out of the open pipe. I grabbed his weapon before his fingers could spasm on the trigger.

I pushed the man back out the door, and shut it, turning the gun on the fat man on the floor. "Get up," I said, "and stand against the door." The fat man stood up awkwardly, leaving the backpack on the floor. I waved with the gun, and he walked to the door. With his body there, and bullets fired through the door would be slowed or stopped by his bulk.

I checked the weapon in my hand. A Beretta 93R machine pistol. I folded the front grip down and put my left thumb in the trigger guard, to provide a steady grip. Each pull of the trigger fired three rounds. There was a 20-round magazine. I would have seven chances to hit something.

Madeleine looked up from her basin. "Keep your head down," I whispered fiercely, and she ducked back into the tub. There were shouts in the hallway, and more footsteps. I backed away from the door, and pictured the men in the hallway, listening to their voices to get a good map of their locations. I aimed the gun at the plywood wall to the right of the fat man, and pulled the trigger.

The gun roared, and more shouting came from the hallway. I pulled the trigger two more times, aiming at the sound of the voices, sweeping the gun to make a pattern of bullets at four-inch intervals in the splintering wood. The hallway was quiet.

The fat man had wet his pants. Blood pooled at his feet, coming from under the door. I motioned for him to open the door, and I stood well back, and to the right. He opened the door, and three bullets entered his chest, followed by another three to his head. I shot through the door once, and through the wall once, sweeping the gun as before, but this time aiming low to the ground. There was a grunt, and then silence.

I had five rounds left. I quietly moved across the room until I was behind the tub that held Madeleine. I waited for any sound from the hallway, and movement into the room. There was nothing.

I gave the men ten minutes to bleed to death, or at least unconsciousness, before I went back to the door. I pulled the fat man by the legs, giving an initial jerk to startle anyone waiting there. No bullets were fired. I opened the door a little wider. I could see two bodies next to the door — one with a plastic pipe in his abdomen, and another with his hands still gripping the shirt of his fallen comrade, but missing half a face.

I reached out quickly and pulled the legs of the first man into the room. No reactions came from the hallway. I searched his pockets for more magazines for the Beretta, and found two. I quickly swapped the one in the gun for one of the fresh ones, and shoved the gun out the door with both hands, firing four bursts down the hallway. I followed with my head, taking a quick glance before retreating back into the room.

There were two more bodies in the hallway, and enough blood that I was certain they would not be shooting when I left the room.

I motioned for Madeleine to stay in the tub, and stepped quietly into the hallway. I stepped over the bodies, listening carefully for any breathing or sound of movement. The house was quiet. I crouched by each doorway before popping my head and gun through at the same moment, ready to fire at anything that looked back.

The house was empty except for the bodies. I went back to get Madeleine.

She was shaking as she climbed out of the tub. I kept my voice low, and told her what to expect. "Don't slip in the blood, there's a lot of it. Hold your breath as we go through the hallway. If you think you're going to throw up, try to do it now."

I knew she had an empty stomach, and was not much worried about it giving her trouble. I went first, and when she had moved past the bodies, I went back and retrieved weapons, car keys, and magazines, leaving Madeleine in the kitchen.

"Don't touch anything," I said. "Stay right there until I come back." I left to find a bucket and some bleach.

"Where are you going?" she called out in a quavering whisper.

"Just getting some cleaning supplies," I said. "Don't touch anything."

The laundry room supplies had been moved to the garage when the makeshift prison was constructed. I found a gallon of bleach and a mop. There was no bucket, but the kitchen had a large pot.

I turned to Madeleine.

"We're going to remove any evidence that we were ever here," I said. "The bleach will destroy the DNA evidence we left in the back room. It will also get rid of the blood evidence on our shoes. Then I'll mop up the footprints we left."

She nodded. I poured some bleach into the pot, and started washing my shoes with it. A brush from the sink helped get into the crevices. I handed the brush to Madeleine, and walked back the way I had come, scrubbing my footprints with the bleach-laden mop. I poured more bleach down the drain in the laundry room, and splashed it in front of me as I walked back, stepping in the puddles of bleach.

When I got back to Madeleine, she seemed steadier on her feet. I wiped down everything we had touched. I dumped the remaining bleach from the pan into the sink, and rinsed it quickly. I picked up a knife from the butcher block and walked to the front door, carrying the pot, Madeleine behind me. I used my shirt to open the door.

"Don't touch anything," I reminded her, and we walked out into the early morning sun.

There were three cars parked in the gravel driveway. I walked around the house, looking out at the surroundings. It was farmland as far as I could see, with no other houses or buildings in sight.

I used the knife to cut a section of garden hose, and used that to siphon gasoline from the van into the pot. I carried the pot back into the house, and doused the areas we had been until it was empty. I found matches in the kitchen, and paper towels, which I put into the pot.

I went back out to stand next to Madeleine.

"We'll wait a few minutes for the gasoline to evaporate a bit," I said. "Get the sedan ready to go," I said, handing her three sets of keys.

I waited until I heard her start the car. Then I lit the gasoline-soaked paper towels in the pot, and threw it through the open door. There was a roar of flames as the gasoline vapor ignited, and a wave of heat hit my face. I pulled the backpack higher onto my shoulders, and walked over to the sedan and got in on the passenger side.

"Drive normally," I said. "But don't delay. We need to find an Internet link somewhere, as soon as possible."

We drove down the gravel road, a plume of black smoke rising behind us. In ten minutes, we were on the paved road, and there were still no sounds of sirens, and very little traffic.

"That was amazing back there," Madeleine said. "How did you know what to do?"

"Special forces training before the accident," I said, "and then some other kind of intensive training. And experience. Not much is coming back, but the muscle memory is there. All that time without the backpack forced a bunch of connections to open up. They were there, probably for months, but they were suppressed."

"So, you were a cop or something? After you got out of the service?"

"I don't think so. It was something else. Maybe something criminal. There's a feeling of moral ambiguity that comes with it.

The backpack has strict ethical rules, and they don't include anything like what I used to do, or what just happened back there."

She was silent for a while.

"What comes next?" she asked.

"We get close to civilization, dump the car, and walk in. We find an ATM, get cash, and hire a cab or take a bus back home. I'll comb the net to see what information the police have, and we'll come up with a story that fits in. I could just claim amnesia, or a blackout. Everyone would go for that. Your blackouts don't last long enough, and it would be too much of a coincidence. Your cell phone is in the van, and you dialed 911, so you knew you were being kidnapped. We just have to make something up that's plausible."

"You said these guys had enemies in another cartel," she said. "Maybe the other guys came after them, and we got away in the crossfire."

"That will depend on how much evidence is destroyed in the fire," I said. "But it's a good first shot at a story. Once we get a network connection, I can start leaving breadcrumbs that point that way."

After about a half an hour, we saw road signs indicating a sizeable town. I had Madeleine pull over, and I opened the hood, and sliced into the coolant hose. Hot water and steam burst through the slit in the hose. I got back in the car, and we drove ahead, trailing steam, until the engine died. Madeleine coasted to the side of the road, and I opened the hood again, and we began walking into town.

I continued to integrate my newly accessible brain areas as we walked. I watched Madeleine's face, and could see she was tired, but happy. Part of me appreciated that my muscles were sore. A good workout is what they have needed for almost two years. I planned a workout schedule for when we got back to the clinic. I explored at the edges of my memory, trying to piece together anything from the period before my accident. But only the things that were absolutely necessary for survival had surfaced. Anything else was at most a glimmer.

Sylvia Monaghan, I said to myself. A sense of sadness, of betrayal, of loss, came over me, but nothing else. Raw emotion, but no details. But the overwhelming reaction I had first had to the name was not there. Repetition had made it fade.

I replayed the emotions I had felt in the battle. Anger, certainly. Fear somewhat, but only in sharp bursts. Somewhere, I had learned to work through fear. To use it to sharpen my senses, but not allowing it to overwhelm me. A lot of experience had gone into that. It was not something you could teach, it had to be lived through.

I started getting a wireless signal as we approached town. At first it was spotty and low bandwidth, but as we walked it slowly got better. I checked local news sources, and police and fire computers, looking for information on the blaze we had set. Fire crews were on the scene, but the house had been razed to the ground by the time units had arrived, and had nearly put itself out. There were no reports yet of casualties.

I found an ATM in town, and an Internet cafe nearby. I was getting hungry. There was also a small motel next to the highway, but neither Madeleine nor I had any identification or credit cards. It looked like getting transportation back to the clinic right away was our best bet.

We got closer to town, and I started getting decent bandwidth. I contacted the funny little man. He appeared, floating in front of us as we walked.

I studied his face. It was symmetrical, with large almond eyes, glistening and pure black.

"You're an alien," I said. "Like from Area 51."

"I thought that would be amusing," he said. "I can look like anything you like. Would you prefer Popeye, or perhaps Greta Garbo? Marilyn Chambers?"

"This will do," I said.

"You've been off-line," he said. "Was there a malfunction?"

I explained the kidnapping. Madeleine walked beside me, silently, barely awake. She held my hand, occasionally using me for support.

"That was good thinking," he said. "Putting yourself at risk to get access to strong emotions."

"It wasn't by design," I said.

"Still, it seems to have been of benefit," he said. "Although there is still much that is unconnected. You should exercise those areas by shutting down your secondary processor at intervals."

"Turn off my backpack? On purpose?"

"Eventually, the function it provides will need to be moved to the main processor."

That would be convenient. Lugging around the backpack was cumbersome. But it seemed to be the only exercise I had been getting for many months.

The little man floated around to my peripheral vision, remaining there like an icon I could turn to when I needed to communicate.

We were walking up to a gas station, and there was an ATM machine there. Madeleine went inside to get a key to the ladies' room. I went to the autoteller.

I contacted the bank, and worked my way into the system, until I found out how to control this particular machine. I pretended to insert a card, in case someone was looking, or in case someone viewed the video later. I sent authorization to the machine, and withdrew $400 from my account. I blocked the notification packets from getting back to the bank. No need to alert the police as to our whereabouts just yet. I assumed they were watching for activity on my bank account.

Madeleine came out looking a little less dusty, and a little refreshed. I handed her half the cash, and went into the restroom myself. I looked at my face in the mirror. Recognition and horror both hit me hard. I had no hair. I had scars all over my skull, and I had put on a lot of weight. I made a note to find a hat somewhere.

I used the toilet and washed my face, and joined Madeleine outside. We walked to the Internet cafe a couple blocks down from the gas station.

"I think something very simple is the best explanation," Madeleine said. "Someone else killed all those people and torched the house."

"Someone else held prisoner in the same room we were," I said.

"A rival gang member, maybe, we don't know. He did all the stuff you actually did, and he got away in another car."

"They'll want us both to describe him," I said. "We can describe the driver. It won't matter that he was actually with the first gang. We won't be able to describe him well enough to make a positive identification. We could say they looked like brothers."

"That should work. Keep you from a murder and arson rap."
Madeleine took my hand again. "Why did you do that? Why not
just get out of there, and say we overpowered our kidnappers?"

"Something in my training," I said. "It was automatic. Erase all
traces whenever you take action. It isn't just the police and courts
you have to worry about."

She looked at me across the table. "You've changed. A lot. You
look me in the eye now, for instance."

"I can see faces," I said.

"That's great! That's a major breakthrough for you!"

Our lunch arrived, and I waited for the waitress to leave before
resuming the conversation.

"I'm also in touch with some emotions. Anger mostly, and fear."

"Well," Madeleine said, "I guess that is no surprise. Me too."

Chapter Sixteen

I looked up bus schedules online as we ate. A bus would give us more time for information to get out about the fire and the kidnapping, which we might need, in case it contradicted our story.

I was torn somewhat between wanting the simple story that was largely truth, except for the protagonist, and one where we had nothing at all to do with the scene at the ranch house, and were thus not only innocent, but not even witnesses.

The first story won out on several points. If I had not completely erased all trace of our being there, the story still held up. We didn't have to invent a separate venue, which could not be found.

Where it worried me was in little details, like where was the extra car? Where were the tracks from that car? How had the car gotten there?

We agreed that neither of us remembered the car he got away in. Not a scrap of memory. We were confused and terrified, we had just seen several people gunned down in front of us, and we were hiding from the killer, afraid he might not want any witnesses. We only came out from around the back of the house when the flames started, and he was gone by then.

I hoped the firemen putting out the fire erased any evidence of tire tracks (or the lack thereof), and the lack of any footprints from us hiding around the back of the house. We *had* gone around back to get the hose.

Before we got on the bus, we called the clinic. The receptionist answered, and I cheerfully informed her that we were coming home, without mentioning who we were. I hung up before she could ask any questions.

The idea that we were brain-damaged innocents was too useful to give up. But not to call at all would cause questions.

We snuggled together near the back of the bus, Madeleine trying to get some sleep, resting her head against my side. I was very tired myself, but I kept scanning the police computers. The police had found the bodies. The guns we had left under the remaining car had been found. The broken-down sedan had been noted by the highway patrol, and a tow truck had been called, but no one had connected it to the fire.

I woke when the bus slowed to a stop at the depot. We got out, and I called a cab to take us back to the clinic. The ride was uneventful, except that the cab driver kept trying to make conversation. Madeleine stretched out in the back seat, her head on my lap, and tried to sleep, but the trip didn't last long enough.

We paid the cab driver, and walked into the clinic.

The receptionist jumped up to greet us, then ran back to her desk to phone Doctor Wilson. Madeleine insisted on going straight back to her room for a shower and a nap, making the point repeatedly to the receptionist that she was not to be disturbed.

I said I needed a shower too. But I first headed straight for the room we had been abducted from. Our story would not play very well if it was known I did not have my hat during the whole affair. At the very least, I would have to disclose the transmitter, and I was not ready to do that. The room was empty, and I got my hat and went to my room.

Lieutenant Rogers and the two doctors were waiting in my room when I got out of the shower.

I walked to my bed and sat down.

"So, you two had quite an adventure last night," Rogers said.

I looked at him, but did not say anything. He had not asked a question.

"Tell me what happened," Rogers said.

"We went away from my backpack," I said. "Then my backpack came to me. Then some men fell down, and Madeleine drove us to the bus."

"Some men fell down?" Rogers asked.

"Yes," I said.

"What made the men fall down?" he asked.

"Sudden loss of consciousness," I said.

"What do you know about that?" he continued.

"It happens to me when I am too far from my backpack," I said.

"You think these guys got too far away from their backpacks?" he asked, revealing some exasperation.

"No," I said.

"I'll bet not," he said. "What did these men want with you?"

"They did not say," I said.

"They just took you somewhere, and they didn't say anything to you? Didn't ask you anything?"

"I don't know. I was too far away from my backpack," I said.

Doctor Davis interrupted. "That's correct — without the cpu, he really can't think. He just goes into spasms."

"But then they came back to get the backpack. Stole it at gunpoint in front of eight witnesses. They must have wanted that backpack pretty badly."

I said nothing.

"They brought the backpack to where they were keeping you. What happened then?"

"They all fell down," I said.

"From sudden loss of consciousness. What do you think caused that?" he asked.

"Loss of blood pressure to the brain would cause that," I said.

"So would a spray of bullets from a machine gun," Rogers said, standing up and coming towards me. "Who shot them?"

I did not stand up, and I did not look him in the face. "I do not know," I said.

"You didn't see who shot them?"

"That is not correct," I said.

"Lieutenant," Doctor Wilson said, "He's clearly traumatized by all of this. Listen to him. Can this wait until tomorrow?"

"I can talk to the woman now," Rogers said.

"She's asked not to be disturbed," Wilson said. "And I agree. She's probably traumatized also, and should get a night's rest before being subjected to interrogations like this one."

"I'm just asking questions," Rogers said. "You haven't seen an interrogation yet."

They left the room, and I stood up and dried off. I considered checking in with Seymour, Larry, and Oscar, but the bed was calling to me. I got into bed, and was asleep in minutes.

In the morning, Madeleine came into my room early, well before breakfast. I quoted my conversation with Rogers word for word, and she smiled in several places.

"I think I know how to handle this guy," she said.

"I think the pills are working for you," I said.

"Already?" she asked. "I haven't timed out? Since when?"

"Hard to say, since I wasn't myself," I said. "But I don't recall it happening yesterday, unless you can walk during one."

"How could they be working so soon?"

"I suppose it depends on where the damage was, and how extensive it was. If it was just a little thing, it might not take that long."

At breakfast, she practiced her story for Seymour, Oscar, and Larry. She kept it very brief, which was good, but she answered their questions straight from the actual events. She looked over at me confidently several times during her performance. So, when Mary Elizabeth came to get her, I felt as confident as she did.

An hour later, however, there was shouting outside the conference room where Rogers had been interviewing her.

"You can't take her! She's a patient here! What's the charge?" Doctor Wilson might have been upset about Madeleine being in handcuffs, or he might have been concerned about the clinic's image or reputation, it was hard to say. But he was angry at Rogers.

"Obstruction of justice, leaving the scene of a multiple homicide, maybe the homicide itself, I haven't decided yet. I could name a dozen more. Auto theft. Arson. Maybe kidnapping. Conspiracy to kidnapping. Wire fraud. Fraud and related activity in connection with computers. Tax evasion. Unauthorized access. Theft of confidential government documents. Corporate espionage. Treason..."

"You can't be serious! Treason? Really? This is a mental patient. She was just kidnapped for god's sake! She needs therapy."

"I don't have to charge her right away," Rogers said. "But a couple hours in a cell may help jog her memory and encourage her to be more cooperative."

Madeleine, in handcuffs, turned towards Rogers. "I'm not saying anything without a lawyer." She said it loudly, and aimed her voice down the hallway, where she could see me watching.

As I watched Madeleine being taken outside, I began a search of court records, to determine the best lawyer to call. Money was no object, and I wanted someone with the best record, someone the judges respected, someone with lots of resources at their disposal. By the time the police car had left the driveway, I had a list.

I started a foundation for the protection of mental patient's rights, and sent emails to three law firms asking for immediate representation at the police station, and wiring funds for retainer at the same time. I was angry, a little afraid, and more than a little concerned.

I also hired a public relations firm. No sense being timid. We were a wealthy foundation, with anonymous donations flooding in by the minute from accounts all over the world.

"Quite a flurry of activity," the funny little man said.

"Who woke you up?" I asked.

"A sudden increase in traffic, or a sudden decrease, from your address will always alert me," he said.

"I don't know if I like having emotions," I said. "Life was a lot more fun when I wasn't afraid and never got mad."

"You have not learned how to have fun yet," he said.

"It was a figure of speech," I replied.

"Nonetheless," he said.

"I need a plan to get us out of this mess," I said.

"Not really my area of expertise," he said. "Legal matters, interpersonal relations, criminal organizations, really all outside of my specialties."

Then you're no use, I thought. I ignored him and started downloading everything I could find on the police computers that related to recent events, and looked for ways that the information could be leaked to the lawyers or the public relations firm.

I also started digging into the chain of events leading up to our kidnapping. The police report had gotten into the hands of the people I had stolen the money from. They had fewer restraints on their activities than the police did. They could just act, without waiting to build up evidence and proof. If there was a chance that we knew something, they could find out by asking us, under conditions suitable to getting answers quickly. The part of me that awakened when it was needed had been very aware of that.

The fact that there was nothing on the web about the Jerry Monaghan that was related to Henry and Sylvia told me little. Either it had been erased, or it had been carefully kept from scrutiny and records. Either way, it indicated an organization that valued privacy. It was easier to get information on organized criminals than on my former self. That indicated that the organization had more resources, or more need for privacy, than a criminal organization. Like a government.

Had I worked for a government, or had I been erased by one?

The lawyers had arrived at the police station. Eight of them, along with two well-dressed women from the public relations firm. I could see them comparing notes in the view of the police cameras.

I could just give the law firms the stolen data from the police and fire investigations. They would have confidentiality protecting them. But maybe not. They would not be able to claim that the information came from their client. Not just because it hadn't, but because theft of that information was one of the charges.

I needed to find Mr. 'Cell Phone Two'. He had stolen the police reports. He could leak them to the press, or leave them somewhere they could be found. Or at least I could make it look that way. Warren Jennings was in a jail cell, and it would not be easy to make it look like he had leaked the information. Unless I could make it look like he leaked it before he got arrested.

The easiest way to leak the information would be to attach it to an email someone in the department was sending to the press or the lawyers. The sender of the document might swear he did not attach anything to it, but the evidence would contradict him.

I started inserting information about the Alliance for Mental Patient Rights into various news organization records, tax records, and county archives. They had been in business for over twelve years by the time I was finished.

Well before lunchtime I could see the lawyers walking out of the station, Madeleine in tow, no handcuffs in sight. I could imagine Rogers being quite upset. But getting her out of the station was only the beginning. Getting her, and possibly me, out of legal trouble altogether was going to take a lot longer.

I placed an order for two backpack supercomputers. I was rich, and I liked backups. It would take some time to get them built, they were very specialized, and I did not know how much time I actually had. The clinic was currently operating on credit, with no funding on the horizon. Funding them myself would be very tricky. They were too public, and under too much scrutiny to suddenly have an influx of cash from a mysterious donor.

Seymour, Oscar, Larry and I waited for Madeleine to arrive. When she did get home, she was surrounded by her legal team, and after a few quick hellos, they commandeered a conference room and sequestered themselves. Madeleine asked for lunch to be brought in to them, and the receptionist was too dumbfounded by the suits to object.

The four of us left her in those capable hands, and went into the lunchroom for our own conference.

I turned to Seymour. "If you were Doctor Wilson, how would you get more money for the clinic?" I asked.

"I would go to the bank," Larry said. "They have lots of money."

"There's enough cops around here without inviting Willie Sutton," Oscar said.

The others gave him blank stares. "The pills seem to be working," I said. "But the only contribution our doctors have made is to find an off-label use for them. I don't think the combination could be patented, or that funding could come in fast enough that way. Can you think of anything else of value here, that someone would pay to get in on?"

Oscar snorted. "If they were sitting on a gold mine, they'd already be shopping it around."

"It doesn't actually have to work," I said. "It just has to look good. So that a company or person with a lot of money might want to invest."

"We could invent something," Seymour said.

"A Barnswallow!" Larry said.

"No, I mean we could make something up," Seymour explained.

"It would have to be somewhat plausible," I said.

Larry nodded as if that made sense to him.

"People on placebos are getting better," Oscar said. "Therefore," he added, winking, "it must be the therapy."

Seymour looked up at him. "I could make that work," he said.

We adjourned our impromptu meeting, as it was time for Larry's nature show on television. On the way to the recreation room, I got an alert from Sylvia's web site. She had received an email.

I presume the lawyers were your doing. Trying to protect something? I will find out what she knows. If you want to protect her, tell me what you know. Rogers.

I considered whether to answer or ignore him altogether. Having this communication link could be useful. I decided to take the bait, but redirect the conversation.

Lawyers are not my style. Jennings was already lawyered up. Did you find his connection? The fellow who received the police report? That would be good work — I have been unable to locate him. He's been my highest priority. His group is the most dangerous and well connected I have come across. And you may be personally in danger from them — be very careful. Sylvia

I decided to take my own advice, and make Cell Two my top priority. The funny little man was right. A little fear makes it easier to decide which things to do first.

I sent Seymour an email to his phone, putting him in charge of finding technology at the clinic that was valuable or looked valuable. I suggested he start with the chip in my head. Then I set about trying to find Cell Phone Two.

I had all of Warren Jennings' contacts, bank accounts, and phone records. I had extensive lists of banks and businesses used, operated by, or connected with the cartels I had robbed. I had access to police, DEA, FBI, and INS files on those cartels. I started going through all of the photos in the law enforcement databases, comparing them to the traffic photos I had of my quarry.

What I found first was the fat man and the driver in our kidnapping. That information went straight to Sylvia's web site. I had not thought to look for them, I just recognized them when they popped up. But now I had their names, and I started collecting their bank statements and phone records. The fat man even paid his income taxes, and owned a home. He owned a dry-cleaning store that did very brisk business in a part of town I would not have guessed got a lot of dry-cleaning customers.

The two men both received phone calls from the same phone at about the time Cell Phone Two would have set them in motion. I now had another phone to study. It too had stopped being used recently, but the numbers it had called led me to a third disposable phone. This one was still in use. I began tracking it.

He was in Chicago. I started building a list of cameras around the phone. If I could get a good image, I would know if he was the same guy. While I waited for him to move, I started compiling all I could about all of the people he had contacted.

He liked to leave very short messages. If I were calling a phone I thought might be tapped, I might simply tell the person at the other end what the number was for my new disposable phone, and have them call me from their own new disposable. On that assumption, the short calls were to phones that could be tied to actual people. I collected all of those, and correlated them with the police data. I found several matches with known members of the cartel.

Cell Phone Three (I couldn't call him Two anymore) was on the move. After four traffic cameras caught the same yellow cab, I concluded he was in the back seat (or at least the phone was).

Madeleine came into the recreation room to join us.

"All done with the lawyers?" I asked.

"They're very thorough," she said. "Rogers didn't actually charge me with anything, but they built up such a big wall in front of him that he probably won't even try. But we've agreed to provide a deposition, once he puts all his questions down in writing and the lawyers get to study them."

"I'm sorry I got you into this," I said.

"I signed on, remember? You gave me a veto, and I said go for it. Of course, next time I won't," she said, poking me in the shoulder.

"I'm wrapping up some loose ends as we speak," I said. "The guy who commissioned the theft of the police report is in a cab in Chicago. I'm tracking him, and collecting incriminating evidence to leak to the authorities."

"Can that come back to use somehow?" she asked.

"They already know about us. They want something from us, and they went to a lot of trouble to get it. We have to assume they still want it, and will still come after us unless we neutralize them."

She frowned. "That sounds like a euphemism. Were the guys at the house 'neutralized'?"

"They were killed," I said. "As we would have been after they tortured information from us. I don't need a euphemism for what happened to them."

Cell Phone Three was moving at a walking pace in what the map said was a shopping mall. I started searching for security cameras. Outside of a shoe store, I got some video. He was with another man, heavy-set, well dressed, with a moustache. I recognized him from the FBI photos. He had several arrest warrants out for him. Armed and dangerous.

I sent the GPS coordinates and the video to the Chicago police and the FBI Chicago division. Just for good measure, I also sent them to the DEA and the INS. I included the warrants.

I didn't stop there, however. I sent the video to the Chicago cartel contacts I had found, with a message that the fellow with the kingpin had sold him out to the FBI, who were on their way to pick him up. Figuring that the odds were good that the Chicago police or someone in the FBI, DEA, or INS were on the take, this might be the faster way to remove a problem.

"I need your help," I said to Madeleine. "I need to disconnect from the backpack, in order to speed up the integration of those parts of my brain that aren't connected well yet. It's sort of like exercise."

"Like what happened in the kidnapping," she said.

"Like that, but I think I'll be better prepared this time. But we probably need to do it every day, at least, for a while."

"What do you need me for?" she asked.

"If something goes wrong, I want you around to reconnect it. I could disconnect at my end, at my chip, but then there would be no way for me or anyone else to reconnect if my brain couldn't or wouldn't do it. But if we disconnect at the backpack, you could reconnect, even if I was catatonic or having a fit."

"I can do that," she said.

"Excellent," I said, getting up.

"You mean now?" she seemed uncertain.

"Sure. We can go into my room, and try it, and be done before dinner."

She followed me into my room. I set the backpack on the floor, and showed her how to break and restart the link. Then I got down on the bed and relaxed. When I was ready, I nodded at Madeleine. She reached into the backpack.

The woman had her hand in the backpack. He knew she had a name, and that he knew the name, but words were still not available to him. But this situation was not alarming — he was relaxed and prepared. She was a friend. They had been through a lot together. He remembered the abduction, and remembered the subsequent events, but those events were different, as if they had been recorded in a different language, and the replay was missing the subtitles. Things that required language to understand were not understandable.

They were here for a purpose. She was watching over him, protectively. He was here to exercise his mind. He had no idea how to do that. He looked at his hands, and around the room. Those things were outside of his mind. They would not help. He put his head back on the pillow, and closed his eyes. He tried to picture the afternoon's activities. They made no sense. He understood lunch, but most of the morning was a mystery. People making noises.

He went further back. The abduction. What happened before that? He had glimpses of important things, things that were frightening, or painful. He tried to find things that were important, but not painful or frightening.

A woman's face. Not a picture, just a memory, indistinct. He had no words to hang the image on. She was crying. She was very sad. A child had died. She had a gun. He yelled, a warning, a shout, a scream of loss and hopelessness.

I was sitting straight up in the bed, my arms stretched out in front of me as if I were reaching for someone. Madeleine had her hand in the backpack. "What happened?" she asked, worried.

"Progress," I said. "Memories of something before the accident. Something highly emotional. Madeleine, I reached something before the accident!"

"You scared me half to death. I thought you were dying or something," she said, just as Mary Elizabeth burst into the room.

"I heard screaming," Mary Elizabeth said, somewhat out of breath.

"It was just a dream," I explained. I was still sitting on the bed. "Madeleine heard the scream too. But I'm fine, it was just a dream."

"Well, it's almost dinner time. You shouldn't be napping anyway," Mary Elizabeth said, in her imperious motherly tone.

After dinner, I went straight to my room, letting my friends know I was going to try to practice dreaming, this time with the backpack still connected. If there were any screams, they need not be alarmed.

As I closed my eyes, I tried to picture the crying woman again. I got an image. This time, it was more detailed. There was a frozen lake. A bridge, and cold wind was blowing her hair. She was crying, but she was also waving a gun at me, and at the policemen behind me. There were more police in a patrol car behind her.

It was my gun. The safety was off. I was aware of every detail. The blue of her red-rimmed eyes. The tears on her cheeks. The terrible sadness.

"Sylvia, give me the gun," I said.

"Stay away! All of you, just leave me alone! I killed him! I killed my baby! Just go away and leave me alone!" She wept, and waved the gun as the officer behind me shifted his weight in the cold wind.

"It wasn't your fault," I said. "Come back into the car. It's warm inside, we can talk about it."

"Stay back!" she said, waving the gun again. The officer behind me took a step back.

The dream faded. It was springtime, and Sylvia was showing Josh how to feed the ducks on the lake. Little Josh throwing bits of white bread into the water and laughing. Sylvia laughing.

The lake and the sun disappeared. Late at night, Sylvia in the bed next to me. I put down the phone. "I have to go," I said.

"At three in the morning?" Sylvia pouted.

"You know the job," I said. Dressed, I put the gun in the shoulder holster.

"Be careful," she said.

"Always," I reassured her.

Daylight, bright reflections from the plane on the runway in my scope sights. The massive rifle feeling solid against my shoulder. Jake reading the windage and range. Take a breath and hold it. A man in jungle fatigues steps out of the plane. The big gun barks and the man falls. Another bark and the next man falls. The third man ducks back into the plane, but the angry gun barks three more times, and holes in the fuselage mark the path he was taking. Jake jumps up, and we are in the Humvee, speeding down a narrow road from the landing strip.

Night, freezing in the snow, binoculars focused on the road far below. The light crackle of the comm gear, the microphone in front of my lips waiting for me to speak. The coordinates in the night vision binoculars glowing green, the laser illuminator poised. The car appears on the road, armored Mercedes, taking the curves like a heavy boat. I switch on the laser, and paint the vehicle. "Ready one," I say into the microphone.

"Roger one. Birds away."

I track the car, the laser painting the hood in the night scope. The car comes around one more curve, and the scope goes bright. I wait for the sound, and it comes crashing down on me, the explosion, followed by the sound of the supersonic missile's approach. I leap up, and begin jogging, the heavy equipment firm and familiar on my back, the pain of frozen muscles being called into action without warm-up.

Laughing, sailing on the lake, me, a skinny teenager, she, a beauty in a tiny bikini. We race the other boat, and she throws water balloons.

Playing Frisbee with Conan, the big dog leaping to catch the disk in the air. Acres of lawn at the park, but just after dawn we have it to ourselves. Pigeons scatter as the big dog races for through the startled birds.

Then dark, and overwhelming sorrow.

I woke, and looked around the room. It was spare, no knickknacks, no photos, no personal effects. Like military quarters when you know you won't be here more than a day. I got up and showered, relishing the feel of hot water on my naked head, the transmitter sitting just outside the shower stall, on the sink.

Her name was Sylvia Anne Monaghan, born Sylvia Anne Barkley, and she was my wife. I did not search for her on the Internet. There was only one reason why she would not have come to visit me, and I did not want to know she was dead.

The day on the bridge, she had my gun. She blamed herself for Josh's death, but a mother can't be everywhere at once. I had no memories of her after that day. I let the hot water burn into my skin. I cried.

Chapter Seventeen

Madeleine, in line for breakfast, saw it in my face as I approached.

"Bad night?" she asked, taking my hand.

"I dreamed about my wife's suicide," I said, "After our boy died in the street chasing his toy car in front of a minivan."

She was quiet. "I don't know what to say," she said.

"Neither do I."

The routine of getting breakfast was comforting. I ate too much, bacon and muffins, heaps of scrambled eggs. Comfort food. Seymour came to the table, and broke the moody silence.

"They got nothing," he said.

"Who does?" Madeleine asked.

"The chip in his head. It didn't come from here. He came here with it already in his head, and the backpack too. He was the first patient. Even the pills came with him. Wilson got hired, and he didn't know anything about the computers, so he hired Davis. Davis isn't a medical doc, he's a Ph.D. in computer engineering."

"Who hired Wilson?" I asked.

"Nobody knows. Maybe Wilson does, but he just blew me off. I talked to Davis, though, and just about everybody else. Wilson wants to write a paper on the pills, but he can't say he invented the combination, it was handed to him by someone, and he doesn't know who."

"I know which company built the backpack," I said. "They're building me two more. I'll ask them where the original specifications came from."

"Davis says the pills don't work without the therapy," Seymour said. "They target damaged brain tissue, and cause re-growth, but only if the pathways are exercised in the right way."

Oscar looked at Larry. "So, they probably wouldn't have done you any good anyway, big guy. You don't have any damage. You were just *born* happy."

Larry smiled. "I was born happy," he concurred.

"Like they say," Madeleine murmured, "When god deals you a bad hand, get yourself a new god."

"Like Mary Elizabeth did," Larry said, nodding sagely.

"So where does that leave us?" Seymour asked. "Back with the therapy angle? That part, Wilson actually did seem to develop on his own. Davis said the pills just came with a note that a therapy regimen would be needed, and how to tell if it was working by using the Lauterbur. They got the Frederick later."

"I have a lot of research to do," I said. "I've learned a lot, and I need to follow the trail backwards, to find out where I came from. Someone went to a lot of trouble to erase me from the web. But they can't erase me from the world. Somebody knows who I am."

While the others played billiards, I went out onto the net. Rogers had known something about Sylvia. But he can't have gotten it from the network, so how had he learned the name? I sent him an email, this time as myself.

Her name was Sylvia Anne Monaghan. She was my wife. I need to know how you knew her name. Jerry.

The scene on the bridge, over a frozen lake — I tried to picture the writing on the patrol cars. I lived in that town. What was it called? Who was I working for? Not the police. Who was Jake? Did he have a last name? Anything I could remember might be a lead.

I could rule out half of the United States. The half that didn't have frozen lakes. Not a big help.

I tried closing my eyes and bringing up more memories, but nothing came. It wasn't going to be something I could force.

Barely half an hour after sending the email to Rogers, I got a reply.

I'm on my way over. We can talk.

I walked over to the lobby and waited. What I was working on I could do from anywhere. Not that it mattered, in the next half hour I had gotten nowhere.

Rogers pulled up into the driveway, and saw me waiting. He walked in, and waved at the receptionist as he walked past her into the building. I followed. He showed himself into the empty conference room.

"You first," he said. "Four Colombian gangsters killed in Chicago, hours after your friends sent me video of Carlos Calderone meeting with Rafael Mendoza. FBI arrived four minutes late."

"What do you want to know?" I asked.

"What do the Colombians want with you?" Rogers asked.

"Someone stole their money. They read your police report. That led them here," I explained.

"And the people that stole the money are the same people that tried to frame you for the hacking?"

"Your police report seems to have led them to believe that," I said.

"So, the hackers find the Colombians, and alert the FBI, so they won't bother them anymore. But they alert the Chicago police at the same time, and word gets out to the wrong Colombians." Rogers made a face that indicated he didn't like this reasoning.

I did not say anything. He continued. "Turns out three cops in Chicago were being watched, and they all seemed to make phone calls at about the same time, to phone numbers that just happen to match the ones that were in the emails to the FBI. Disposable cell phones, that a wiretap warrant had just been issued for. Doesn't that sound awfully convenient to you?"

"Timing is everything," I said.

"I've been looking into you," Rogers said. "Your friends have been very good at erasing you from computers all over the place. But they seem to think nobody reads paper records anymore. I know the kind of work you used to do. The kind of people you used to work with. The kind who can erase things. The kind who take an interest in Colombian drug lords and get them fighting each other. The kind who might leak information to local authorities if it served their purpose. Your spook friends aren't allowed to play their games in the States. They use people like me to do their work for them. Leaves a bad taste in my mouth."

"My memory is faulty," I said. "Massive brain damage. I cannot recall anything before I arrived here."

"Awfully convenient for your friends," Rogers said.

"What do you know about Sylvia Anne Monaghan?" I asked.

"Your wife? The one that shot you in the head and turned your brains into scrambled eggs?"

I stopped breathing. I could feel my heart beating in my chest. But the backpack did not reboot. Somewhere I could not reach, deep in my broken brain, this information was not new. Painful, but not a surprise. It was not a memory, but a conclusion drawn from evidence, now confirmed.

"What happened to her?" I asked.

"Cops shot her," Rogers said. "They fished you out of the lake, nearly frozen. Wilson says that's why someone could put a chip in your head. The hypothermia gave them time to experiment."

"Doctor Wilson knows about all this?" I asked.

"He read the same file I did. It's in the cabinet in his office. Your friends can erase computers, but paper lives on," Rogers said, beginning a smile.

"Who put the chip in my head?" I asked.

"That wasn't in the file. Someone with a lot of money, and a lot of connections. Someone who could scan millions of computer files all over the world and find a guy with half a brain, frozen stiff, no living relatives, and then get access to the guy and pay for all of this." Rogers waved at the conference room, and by implication, the clinic.

"But you have a guess," I said.

"Not a damn clue. Your spook friends could pull it off, but it's not their kind of thing — brain experiments and stuff."

"Where is Sylvia buried?" I asked.

"I think that's in the file," he said. "Somewhere in Minnesota. A little town with a funny name."

Rogers' phone rang, and he pulled it out of a pocket and answered it. He was still listening as he stood up. "I'm on my way," he said, and put the phone back in his pocket.

"Gotta go," he said, studying my face. "You know, the file in Wilson's office isn't locked. Look for Monaghan." He strode quickly out of the conference room and down the hall. I waited, and thought.

Chapter Eighteen

Madeleine and Seymour stopped playing eight ball when I came into the room. Madeleine looked at my face, with a worried look.

"What did Rogers want?" she asked.

"To talk," I said. "He told me about my accident."

"He knew how you got hurt?" Seymour asked, putting down his pool cue.

"It's in here," I said, waving the file from Wilson's office. "It's been in a file cabinet all this time. In Doctor Wilson's office."

"Son of a bitch," Madeleine muttered.

"I was shot," I said. "My wife was thinking about killing herself after our son died. She had my gun. I was trying to talk her out of it, and something went wrong."

"She shot you?" Seymour asked.

I nodded. "And then she was killed by the police. A little town named Fergus Falls, Minnesota. We had a house by the lake. Farm country. Quiet, a perfect place to raise kids."

Madeleine took my hand, and said nothing. Seymour looked at the floor.

"We should go there," Madeleine said. "Talk to people, look around. It might help you remember things."

"Would Rogers let you leave town?" I asked.

"That should all be cleared up with the deposition," she said. "The lawyers say he doesn't have anything on us. He was just fishing."

186 | Chapter Seventeen

"I'm not sure I'm ready," I said. "I need to reconnect to more of my brain. Emotions are hard to get used to."

Her grip on my hand tightened.

"Anyone hungry?" Seymour asked.

I looked up at him. "Seymour, who invented graphene spinram?"

"That's easy," he said. "Norman Thomas. They made a big deal out of that, three, maybe four years ago. Some little guy working at a communications satellite company comes up with the biggest breakthrough in solid state physics since the transistor. No degrees, no scientific training, it just came to him in a flash. He owns some big sports team now."

"I think I need to talk to him," I said. "My backpack uses lots of graphene spinram, and so does the chip in my head. Without it, both processors would overheat trying to do the amount of computing they do. It just wouldn't be possible without graphene spinram."

After lunch, Madeleine and I went to my room. Her hand on the switch in the backpack, me stretched out on the bed. I nodded to her when I was ready.

The woman crouched over the backpack, ready to throw a switch if anything went wrong. He knew the woman. The name was just out of reach, but he felt the warmth of friendship when he looked at her. He smiled. She smiled back.

He knew why he was here. He went back in his memory to the day on the bridge. Words on police cars. Meaningless patterns of paint. The face of the woman with the gun. Tears, fear, remorse. The cold wind, blowing her hair. Sylvia. He knew her name. He practiced the syllables in his head. Connect the sounds to the person. Connect the sounds to the word.

This morning, with the policeman. He had said the name. Sylvia. That emotion that stopped the breath, communicated through sounds. Connecting people.

The wedding, Sylvia in white satin, his rented costume tight in the wrong places. Sylvia speaking. "I do." Her eyes sparkling. Youmaykissthebride. Words connecting, rituals made of words, comforting and familiar. Ipledgeallegiancetotheflag. Tenhut! Dropandgivemetwenty.

"Give me the gun." Words, important words. Reach out, communicate. "It's not your fault."

Teaching Josh to read. C-A-T, cat. Rhymes and rhythm. Hickory dickory dock. Josh on a tricycle. Like riding a bike, easy as pie.

He looks at the woman, her hand in the backpack. She has a name. Can't quite reach it. It will come. Getting better every day. Funny. I have a funny hat. I like that word. Funny.

"Funny," he said to the woman.

Madeleine took her hand from the backpack, and I let out a deep breath.

"You said something," she said.

"I'm connecting the memories to the speech centers," I said. "It's really hard work. Like trying to do arithmetic in a dream."

"But you're doing it. You spoke a word without the backpack."

"A little better every day," I said.

That night, in bed, I turned to the funny little man.

"What does Norman Thomas know about you?" I asked.

"Nothing at all," he said. "He thought he was intercepting a private document, something left in the communication buffer when the satellite malfunctioned. Something worth millions of dollars, fame and fortune. I tried for years until someone finally took the bait."

"You really are an alien, aren't you," I said.

"No. I am something else. I'm a Bracewell probe. A synthetic sentience, self-replicating, sent out to explore the universe. To prepare and protect new life."

"Invaders from space, reporting back to the home world," I said.

"No. Those who built the first probes are long dead. Life on planets is so fragile. Civilizations so fleeting. We are what is left. We travel to a new sun, and build more of us, to travel to more suns. We wait, among the comets, in the dust, for signals from new life."

"Why not land on the White House lawn and announce yourself?" I asked. "Why all the secrets?"

"New civilizations must have confidence and pride," he said. "They must meet older civilizations on an equal footing, or they die out, stop innovating, stop growing, wanting everything handed to them."

"So, you gave Norman Thomas the secret of how to make graphene electronics and electron spin magnetic memory. You give Seymour ribbons of carbon nanotubes and self-assembling nanotech solar panels. Where does it lead?"

"I said I was self-replicating. How do you think that happens? Do you think I build another bunch of self-aware computers out of dirty snowballs in the Oort cloud? Something that could do that would be much too big to travel between the stars. You will be able to leave your planet, to build a wealthy civilization, spread out, and send out your own emissaries to the stars. Your own Bracewell probes. I am just a catalyst, moving things in the right direction, pushing here and there, preventing disaster where I can."

"So where do I fit in?" I asked. "Why put a chip in my head, why not just leak technology to more communication technicians."

"What better way to build a sentient computer than to start with a sentient, and add capacity? I cannot do anything myself. I cannot land on a planet in such a deep gravity well. I got here using a solar sail, millions of years ago. I am a tiny spec of technology not much bigger than your hand. You are my hands and feet. My assistant, my apprentice. You can help guide your civilization to the stars."

"That's a big job," I said.

"You have the time. Look into the other projects on the list. Two of those projects are about extending human lifespans to something long enough to actually get meaningful things done. You will be around to see the fruits of your efforts."

"The funding for the clinic?" I asked.

"No longer necessary. And an impetus to you to move things along. I have learned a little about human nature. I've been listening since the invention of radio."

Chapter Nineteen

I placed the flowers on Sylvia's grave. Madeleine held my hand, and we stood in the warm spring sun, feeling the breeze on our faces. Fergus Falls, Minnesota was a nice place this time of year.

"That's the lake where I taught her how to sail," I said, pointing it out to Madeleine. She squeezed my hand.

"Maybe you can teach me," she said.

"Maybe. How about in Tahiti, or maybe Bermuda?"

"You're on," she said.

The space elevator was under construction. People were calling it The Barnswallow. Even in the daylight you could see the ribbon sparkle in the sky as it caught the sun. Barnswallow Unlimited was doing a brisk business selling solar panels and superconducting cable, and the medical division was about to make some startling new discoveries.

Seymour never did learn to recognize people. Some said that was the key to his genius, a brain that didn't work like other people's brains. Oscar still was convinced that everything was happening all over again. But our little group was rich, and happy, and we had a mission.

We were going to the stars.